The Drowning Bell

Elizabeth Edson Block

Wasteland Press

www.wastelandpress.net
Shelbyville, KY USA

The Drowning Bell
by Elizabeth Edson Block

First Printing – April 2014
Paperback ISBN: 978-1-60047-948-9
Hardback ISBN: 978-1-60047-949-6
Library of Congress Control Number: 2014934709

Printed in the U.S.A.

0   1   2   3   4   5   6   7   8

This book is lovingly dedicated to my children, Nathan and Erin, and to my grandchildren, Connor, Harper, Sam, and Emerson.

CHAPTER ONE

The first time I remember hearing the drowning bell ring was on the evening of my eighth birthday, and it was ringing for me. I wasn't drowned, of course, and after the general joy and relief at my appearing, dry and un-drowned, in the midst of the gathering search-and-rescue team, I was in quite a bit of trouble.

The drowning bell presided over a little grassy rise overlooking the swimming beach on the north shore of St. Luke Lake. The platform supporting the bell was made of fat oak timbers and steel, and the bell itself was a heavy brass affair with the words "Let Freedom Ring" engraved around the rim. Apparently, the bell had originally been ordered as a patriotic shrine, but at some point a need had arisen, and the bell had been pressed into service as an alarm system. It took a grown man to set the bell ringing by leaning on a handle attached to the support beam, and it was only rung when someone was feared to be drowned, or, if luck was with them, to be still in the process of drowning and thus, still eligible for rescue.

Well, that's when it was supposed to be rung. There was the time when two junior high boys, Ronnie Carpenter and Maxie Wernau, had joined forces (and body weight) and managed to set the bell ringing, but when their ill-advised prank was discovered (as it was, almost immediately), the Chief of Police, John Galsworthy, actually locked the boys in jail overnight. As an added humiliation, the boys were released into the custody of their two furious and embarrassed mothers the morning after their short but effective jail term. After news of that episode spread, St. Luke's adolescent population generally left the bell alone.

Anyway, the drowning bell had hung there on the lakeshore for as long as even my father could remember, and he had grown up right across Lake Avenue, the wide elm-lined street that paralleled the shoreline. He guessed that he had heard it rung maybe a dozen times, and he remembered four or five times when somebody had actually drowned. He was to hear the bell rung on two more occasions in that long-ago July, and, both times, it would be ringing for his own child.

Even in 1953, when these events took place, the bell was the most efficient way to gather a crowd of willing rescuers to the scene. It could be clearly heard five or six blocks in every direction, and that meant at least thirty useful people and another thirty useless ones, would be on the scene in a matter of ten minutes or so. Of course, by that time anyone in real danger of drowning had gone ahead and drowned, but if it was just some child adrift in an inner tube, or some shortsighted fellow stuck out in a rowboat without oars, then the situation could be assessed, and someone in the crowd who owned a boat would scoot out and pull them to shore.

In those days, lots of people in St. Luke owned a boat of one description or another. On a summer Sunday you could stand on the end of a dock and watch rowboats, canoes, sailboats, outboards, and even an occasional gleaming Chris Craft go gliding past. In our little Iowa town of 8000 souls, there were a couple of movie theaters, a roller skating rink, and nine or ten churches, but the lake was the center of the town and the chief source of recreation. Most citizens of the time echoed my father in his conviction that anyone who needed a swimming pool for swimming was a little lacking in moral fiber.

Although the drowning bell was only to be heard in times of trouble, its presence there by the shore was a comforting one and the people of St. Luke looked upon it fondly as a protective and benevolent guardian. I have more reason than most for harboring affection for that bell, because twice it rang for me. The first time was about eight o'clock in the evening on July the seventeenth, my eighth birthday. When I awoke to the sound of the bell, I was sitting in the little clay-walled cave in the bluff near our family's wooden dock. Only three people knew about that cave...me, my little brother Charlie, and my best friend Robert. I wasn't deliberately hiding from anyone that evening, but the cave was a good place to go to be alone for a while.

I hadn't set out to cause anyone any trouble, either, but when I'd disappeared from home after supper, and when our good friend and neighbor, Grace Logan, had told my parents that she'd last seen me heading for the lake, and then when my dad had found my empty cowboy boots on the dock, well, then I guess things turned a little frantic. No one had thought to consult Charlie or Robert about where I might have gone to nurse a disappointment.

So there I sat, and when I heard the sound of the drowning bell pealing out through the still evening air, I naturally got pretty curious, so I climbed out of the cave, clambered up the six or eight feet of scrubby clay, and ran the two blocks along the lake bank to where I could see a crowd of anxious people milling around the bell platform. There was an air of general concern, and everyone seemed to be considering what to do next.

The oddest thing was that up there on the bell platform was my very own father. He was talking to the crowd, and he was holding his hand out in front of him, palm down, at about the level of his chest. As I squeezed my way closer I could hear that his voice sounded a little strained, and as I moved closer still, I could make out that he was describing someone.

"She's about this tall, and she's wearing jeans and a cowboy shirt and suspenders. She's barefoot." And then I noticed that in his other hand he was holding my boots and socks. I looked down at my bare feet, realizing suddenly where I'd left those boots.

"That's funny," I thought. "He's describing *me*." I was about four feet tall at the time. I guess I rose up to somewhere between the belt buckle and the breastbone of most of the people in the crowd. I know that once I waded into their midst, I was submerged in a sea of elbows, unable to see out, and invisible to anyone more than two people away. Craning my neck, I looked up at the people closest to where I was standing and spotted Mr. Hibbs, our neighbor from two doors down. I squirmed my way over to him and reached up to tug at his arm.

"Mr. Hibbs? What's going on? How come the bell rang?" Mr. Hibbs looked down at me for a second, then he looked up at my dad, and then he looked down at me again. A look of confusion came over his face as he sorted out the fact of my presence. Then he just seemed to "fluster up" (my brother Charlie's expression), and he took hold of my elbow and started dragging me up through the crowd.

"Bob! Bob!" he was yelling. "She's here! She's here! She's all right! I've got her right here!"

There was quite a stir then, as my unexpected appearance registered with one person after another. My dad jumped down from the bell platform and scooped me up, hugging me and running through six or seven emotions in about fifteen seconds. He didn't seem able to say much...he was kind of teary-eyed and laughing. He sounded a little as though someone had knocked the wind out of him, and he was just starting to get his breath back.

All the people around us had big grins on their faces. They were acting the way people do when their emotions are stronger than they're comfortable with...whacking my dad on the back and saying things like, "She doesn't even look wet, Bob!" and, "You gave your daddy quite a scare, young lady!"

The next thing I remember is my mom scrambling her way through the crowd, dragging my six-and-a-half-year-old brother Charlie. My mother looked as frazzled as I had ever seen her look. She seemed to be struggling to hold back tears, and when she saw me there with Dad, she let out a little yelp of a scream, covered her mouth with her hands, and just folded up right there in the grass.

Well, I was pretty bewildered by all this extreme behavior on the part of adults I'd otherwise known to hold themselves in with a pretty tight rein. Standing there, trying to sort out the situation, I slowly began to realize that the obvious joy at my sudden appearance was probably directly related to my prior *dis*appearance. It further dawned on me that all that joy and celebration were probably soon going to be replaced by some sort of reckoning…something that would compensate all these grown-ups for their anxiety and exertion and general loss of decorum.

The crowd was dispersing in twos and threes, filtering away down the sidewalks and across the lawns. My dad set me down on the grass a minute while he went to my mom, who had risen shakily from where she'd crumpled. Dad patted her on the shoulder a few times, talking in a low voice. Then Mom just leaned up against him, burying her face on his shoulder. Dad gave a little nervous laugh, but he held her there in his arms while she wept out a few shuddery tears of relief.

I was shocked and a little uncomfortable. People's parents simply did not act like that in public, drowned child or not. My brother Charlie was astonished. The whole evening had unfolded for him like the Saturday afternoon movie serial. Glancing suspiciously over his shoulder at our intertwined parents, he walked over to me and stopped. Unlike everyone else, Charlie did not look particularly relieved. He squinted appraisingly, as though he were revising his estimate of me. He had never dreamed that I, or anyone our size, was capable of causing such a commotion. I saw a new respect creep into his expression. He said, "Lizzie, what did you do, exactly?"

I answered honestly, "I'm not sure, but I think I'm gonna get it."

After another minute or so, Mom and Dad came over and took us wearily by our hands. My dad looked down at me and shook his head slowly. "Well, Lizzie, it's been quite a birthday. Let's go home. We'll talk about all this tomorrow."

CHAPTER TWO

My father was right about it having been quite a birthday. Sixty years and more have gone by, and I still remember that day, and the next one, as though they were yesterday, although the memory has taken on the slightly tinted quality of a colorized movie. My eighth birthday, which ended with my not drowning, had started out about fourteen hours earlier. When the six-o'clock chimes rang out from the Presbyterian Church bell tower four blocks from our house, I was floating up and out of sleep and into the soft gold early-morning light of the second-story bedroom I shared with my brother Charlie. Had I been turning six, or even seven, I would have bounded out of bed and clamored around, waking up Charlie and rushing headlong into the day. But I was eight now, and I had learned the art and pleasure of anticipation. So I lay there on my back, my hands behind my head, and I savored the untarnished potential of my birthday.

The room occupied by Charlie and me was a square that jutted out from the north side of the house, so we had both a west and an east window, which meant that light came in from early morning to late evening. The light found comfortable resting places on the polished hardwood floor and the two mismatched oak dressers. Charlie and I slept in chenille-covered twin beds on opposite sides of the room, and the toys and clothes littering the floor formed a bridge between us. We shared the big oak bookcase overflowing with books, comics, and Charlie's Viewmaster picture collection. Dad had made each of us a toy box out of reddish maple and these were tucked into the two outside corners of the room.

The fact that Charlie and I had to share a room didn't seem odd to either of us. Lots of kids we knew shared rooms, often with more than one sibling. And there were, after all, advantages. Charlie was not afraid of lightning and thunder, so he got up and turned on the lights during thunderstorms. I didn't mind having a babysitter, so I lay awake and talked to a petulant and uneasy Charlie on those rare occasions when our parents were out. Lots of things were better with a roommate...Christmas Eve, the nights before vacations, evenings when Mom and Dad hosted bridge club and Charlie and I had to go to bed and miss out on the slightly glamorous ambiance of dressed-up adults who smoked cigarettes and ate bridge mix candy and laughed and played cards until long after my brother and I had fallen asleep.

In fact, Charlie and I co-existed happily. We both led our own lives part of the time, and when our paths did cross, there was rarely friction. I was older by eighteen months and two grade levels, which made me the leader in most situations. I took that role for granted, and Charlie, with his easy nature and good-humored matter-of-factness, seemed equally comfortable operating as a sort of orbiting satellite. On the morning of my birthday, I lay still in my own bed until one lazy "bong" from the church tower told me that fifteen minutes had passed. I looked over at Charlie, and I could see that he was still sound asleep. He was lying on his stomach, his seersucker baseball pajamas bunched up around his neck, his face a little flushed and sweaty, his blond hair stuck to his forehead. One arm hung over the side of the bed, and the fingers of his small, suntanned hand curled against the braided rug on the floor. His breathing was soft and regular, and I knew he really was asleep, because he was a hopeless faker.

I climbed out of bed and tiptoed to the west window, which faced the front of the house. The early morning sun threw long shadows across Cayuga Street. The light picked up sparkles in the sidewalk, and everything seemed green-gold, bright, and welcoming. There was the promise of a beautiful day.

As I watched, our twelve-year-old paperboy, Jimmy Fitzpatrick, turned up our walk. I held very still so I wouldn't catch his eye. I thought, "He doesn't even know I'm here. He doesn't know it's my birthday." It seemed almost odd to me that anyone so close by could be so unaware of the importance of this day in this house. I resisted the impulse to open the window and shout down to Jimmy that I was now eight.

My eighth birthday, I thought, was going to be more than an ordinary birthday, holding more than the ordinary guarantee of a completely self-centered and hedonistic day. First, I was turning eight, which sounded way older than seven…more than just one year older. Eight meant the third grade, where you learned cursive and wrote essays. In the third grade, you no longer had a bathroom right off your classroom. Instead you got to walk down the hall to the third- and fourth-grade girls' bathroom, where you could pick up certain information from the older girls. I knew this because my cousin Mary, who was two grades ahead of me, had told me so. She refused, however, to share with me the actual information. I might tell my mom, and my mom kept in pretty close touch with her mom. I was unconcerned. I assumed it was something to do with making babies, which was all old news to me. My mother had explained the whole process. It all seemed exotic and unreal and totally removed from my life. It was not really something I cared about one way or another.

Some of my girlfriends seemed mildly obsessed with the whole notion of naked boys, but I knew what naked boys looked like. I had caught glimpses of my father in the bathroom, and I saw my brother Charlie's rubbery little penis all the time. He wasn't modest, and he was a slow dresser. I was not especially impressed with the penis as an instrument for urination. I much preferred my own, more streamlined, shape. Except for peeing in the out-of-doors, it just seemed like a better design. For one thing, it didn't flop around and risk getting caught in a zipper, a misadventure my brother Charlie suffered once at the Fairfax County Fair.

He had needed to go, and Mom had taken him into the girls' bathroom with us. He was in a big hurry to get back to the rides and the cotton candy, and Mom, in an effort to help him out, had zipped him right into his zipper. I was four or five stalls away, but I heard the initial yelp and the subsequent teary protests.

But aside from the leap in maturity, there was another reason I was so excited about my eighth birthday. I was almost positive that I was going to get my hunting knife. I had been admiring that knife for weeks. It was on page forty-two of the Outdoorsman catalog, a catalog that ordinarily would have had no place in our home. It was a fat book filled with guns and high-powered bows and deep-sea fishing equipment, and nobody in our house hunted or fished, but the catalog had come unbidden with the outboard motor my dad had bought at a boat show. The knife had a wicked-looking five-inch blade and a fake ivory handle, but the best thing about it was the sheath that came with it. I hadn't even known the word "sheath" until I came upon it in the catalog description, but it was a well-worn part of my vocabulary by the time my birthday rolled around. And if the sheath itself weren't enough, there was a little leather belt that you could use to strap everything to your calf.

The knife had become the centerpiece of dozens of my imaginary adventures in the previous month or two. I had visions of myself fashioning a bow and arrows from tree branches, hacking my way through the tall brush in the vacant lot behind Mrs. Krebb's house, and slicing away the gnarly roots that were always tripping us up on the Indian trails.

The Indian trails were part of the natural habitat of any St. Luke child who lived within walking distance of the lake. Most of the actual shoreline consisted of a skinny little strip of dirty sand cluttered with driftwood and weeds and dead fish, which smelled pretty rank as the summer wore on. From the back edge of the sand a bluff rose up fifteen or twenty feet, and worn into the side of the bluff was an on-again off-again path trampled hard by the feet of fifty-some years' worth of kids. Everyone in St. Luke, including the grown-ups, knew that that path was the Indian trail. The trail was scattered with scrubby bushes and tree roots, and I imagined that, armed with my five-inch blade, I could scrape that trail smooth enough for a bicycle.

As a matter of fact, local history did not recommend the path for bike riding. When my cousin Billy had been in junior high, he'd been riding his bicycle along the sidewalk that bordered the upper edge of the bluff. He was speeding along at quite a clip, when he rounded a corner and found himself bearing down fast on the young and pretty Mrs. Hardy, who was pushing her little girl Cindy in a baby stroller. Billy stepped down hard on his coaster brake pedals, skidded off the side and down the steep slope of the bluff, bumped and crashed along the Indian trail for a little way, and then sailed down the last dozen feet of the cliff, landing on his shoulder and breaking his left arm and his collarbone, and giving a stunned Mrs. Hardy an impressive scare. She later told Billy's mom that she'd been sure he was dead, until she heard him moaning and groaning down on the rocky beach.

Returning to the subject of my birthday...I was really counting on getting that knife. I had been reminding my parents relentlessly for at least a month that what I wanted more than anything was that hunting knife. I left the catalog, opened to page forty-two, on the breakfast table. I left birthday wish lists on my dresser with "hunting knife, page 42," printed clearly at the top. I was dimly aware that it was risky, driving Mom crazy like that, but I couldn't seem to stop myself.

My mom was a patient woman, but about every second day, she would look at me in frustration and say something like, "Oh, Honey, a knife like that is dangerous. It's for grown men—men who go out in the woods and shoot big animals."

And, defiant and irrational, I'd think, "If they *shoot* animals, what do they need a *knife* for?"

Or she'd say, "You know, Lizzie, we'll get you some things you'll like, but they might not be what you expect."

And I would think back to the previous Christmas, when all I'd really wanted was a kitten. My parents had argued, "We don't have a place for a kitten. Kittens ruin the furniture. Kittens are a big responsibility."

Undaunted, I'd countered with, "It can sleep with me. I'll make it a scratching post. I'll take care of it all by myself."

The argument had gone back and forth, but ultimately my parents had insisted, "No kitten."

And then on Christmas Eve, after Charlie and I were asleep, my dad had walked over to our friends the Shaeffers' house and picked out a little orange boy kitten from the litter of six produced by the Shaeffers' cat, Cucumber, two weeks before Thanksgiving. Cucumber, my dad later reported, didn't seem unduly distressed, still having the company of five of her kittens as well as the dog, Armorall, and the rabbit, Four-on-the-floor. (My dad had commented to Mike Shaeffer that it must be time-consuming...calling for a rabbit whose name was so long, but Mike had replied that that was never the problem since the rabbit was always underfoot already. What *was* problematic was cussing it out. The rhythm was just all wrong.)

And so, remembering the previous Christmas morning, when I'd awakened to the little mewling sounds at the foot of my bed, I was pretty confident that, in spite of my mom's denials and my dad's silence on the subject, they would nonetheless come through with the much-coveted knife. On that early morning of my birthday, I turned from the window, padded softly past the sleeping Charlie, and, silent as my seven-month-old cat Edmund Hillary (he was a climber), I crept along the upstairs hall and down the maple staircase.

Though our front door faced west, the two-story entryway had windows on the south, and on summer mornings the early light streamed through the windows and ricocheted up and down the staircase, turning the burnished maple the color of dark honey. Light splashed over the polished banister, the big maple wardrobe, and the worn hardwood floor. Dust motes floated everywhere, like a storm of golden glitter in a snow globe.

Until I was six, I had subscribed to the notion that I was the only person to whom those dust motes were visible. They seemed brushed with just enough magic that I'd believed them discernible only to me. Then one afternoon I'd been sitting by myself on the stairs, spellbound by the specks of floating light, and my mom had squeezed by me carrying a load of laundry. She had stopped a minute, looking down at me fondly. "Whatcha doin', Sweet Pea?"

I'd debated whether or not to reveal my secret vision to her. Experience had taught me that sharing fantasies with grown-ups, even grown-ups who loved you, was not always the best course. I was concerned that Mom might find me a little deluded, or maybe I feared that confiding would diminish the enchantment.

The desire to confide won out over the desire to preserve, and I confessed that I'd been watching little gold flakes drifting in the air. To my astonishment she responded breezily, "Oh, those are called dust motes. They are pretty, aren't they!"

Dust motes looked different to me after that. They had a label now, and they were no longer part of my secret life. They were still pretty, but it was as though someone had revealed to me that leprechauns were indeed real, but that they walked around in suits and ties and went to the office every day.

CHAPTER THREE

On that morning of my birthday, I tiptoed into the front room and curled up on the sofa. The Outdoorsman catalog was on the end table, and I slid it over to my lap. With the ease of much practice, I opened the pages to the picture of my hunting knife and gazed at it in the happy certainty that the blade would be strapped to my leg by the end of the day.

After about ten minutes, I heard the slow, sleepy waking-up voices of my mom and dad. Their bedroom was behind the two double doors off the living room in a room that wasn't really supposed to be a bedroom. My mother had explained to me that, about fifty years earlier, people had three or four living rooms in a row, all designated by different titles and enjoying slightly varying functions. There might be a parlor, a morning room, a drawing room, as well as a formal living room. My parents' bedroom had been such a room in former, more elegant times, but my mother had fallen in love with the big windows in it and had converted it into their bedroom.

As I watched, the big double doors slid open, and my dad's stubbly face appeared. He looked up and saw me grinning at him from my perch on the couch. He stared for a minute, taking in the sight of me, the open catalog, and the earliness of the hour. Then he asked with great solemnity, "Is there something going on today?"

I was, of course, fairly giddy with anticipation. I flew at him and wrapped myself around his middle. "You know! You know! When do I get my breakfast present?"

My mom and I had worked out a detailed birthday schedule the week before. I would get one present at breakfast, a second one at lunch, then go to the matinee with Charlie and my best friend Robert, possibly go out to supper, and then come home for cake and one final present. The plan was calculated to stretch the happiness out over the entire day. My family was very big on birthdays.

Knowing how these things worked, I was fairly sure that the knife would be the last present. Grown-ups, at least the kind of grown-ups who inhabited my world, seemed sold on the idea of saving the best for last. I thought this a risky philosophy, but chose not to debate it. As I looked down the bright smiling path of the day ahead, the distance from first to last didn't seem all that great, and besides, I was within one Cheerios bowl of my first present.

I took my dad's hand and dragged him toward the kitchen in order to set things in motion. "Is Charlie up?" he asked.

In answer, we heard the "Thump, thump, thump, thump, thump, thump, thump, THUD!", that indicated Charlie had run down the first seven steps, paused on the lower landing, and jumped over the last five steps to the floor. He came through the living room to the kitchen, stopping when he saw me.

"How come you're up?" he demanded. Charlie usually got up about six, and I usually arose around eight.

"Geez, Charlie, it's my birthday! How could you forget that?"

But Charlie had lost interest in the conversation immediately after asking his question and had turned his attention to his breakfast. Dad was calmly, efficiently assembling spoons, bowls, cereal, and sugar and placing them neatly on the table. Then he calmly, efficiently, and neatly began to make a pot of coffee. My father did everything calmly, efficiently, and neatly, and I usually found it fascinating, admirable, and calming, but that day I found it a little maddening.

By this time my mother was emerging from the bedroom, tying the belt of her robe and pushing her feet into her slippers as she went. "Hi. Where's the paper?" she said, and she settled into a chair and reached for the Wheaties.

I ran out for the paper, but then found myself surrounded by silent and oblivious cereal-eating, coffee-drinking, newspaper-perusing people doing all the ordinary things in ordinary ways. It was, naturally, driving me crazy. Extraordinary days ought to be extraordinary in every way, but I guess it is pretty difficult to squeeze a celebration into a bowl of cereal.

I knew I wouldn't get my breakfast present until everyone was done eating, so I wolfed down my Cheerios, hoping to somehow reduce the average eating time. After that I had five or ten long minutes of watching Charlie eat. He always spooned in his cereal slowly, biting down on the spoon just a little and making a slurping sound, and one or two dribbles of milk would ooze down his chin. Lift-open-clink-slurp-drip. Lift-open-clink-slurp-drip. He ate this way without ever looking at the spoon. He stared straight ahead, reading the back of the cereal box, hardly blinking.

I sat there watching him as long as I could stand it, but finally I blurted out, "If I read the box to you, could you speed it up a little?"

A soft chuckle issued from behind the Des Moines Register. My father drank his coffee and read his paper with that same unhurried deliberation that he did everything else, and his son Charlie ate his cereal the same way. After what seemed like hours had elapsed, my father leaned back, folded his newspaper, and said, "Well, Mudder, what do we have for the little lady?"

My mom suppressed a grin. (Not necessarily a good omen, I thought.) She got up and went to the cupboard over the stove. Standing on her tiptoes, she fished around a little with both hands and then withdrew a small rectangular package wrapped in cowboy wrapping paper. Handing me the box, she said, "Hope you like 'em, Honey!"

I tore the wrapping off, pried open the folded-in corners of the box top, and pulled out the tissue-enfolded contents. Then I stared in bewilderment. Socks? And not just ordinary socks, but frilly little Sunday school socks with lace ruffles around the tops. I had a moment of anxiety, followed by a dilemma. The socks might be a joke, in which case I could just laugh and demand my *real* present. On the other hand, what if the socks were a serious gift? Did my mom think that, now that I was eight, I would appreciate something more dressy and feminine?

I sat there, nervously fingering the ruffles, mentally preparing my response. I glanced up at my parents from under my eyebrows and searched for clues in their faces. I detected a grin struggling behind my father's bland expression, and then a laugh erupted, and then my mom started to laugh, and relief swept over me. "Why, Lizzie! Don't you like them?" my father teased.

Charlie, still eating cereal and dribbling milk, looked blankly from one of us to the other.

I was getting inpatient. "C'mon, you guys, you didn't waste my breakfast present on *socks*, did you?"

At that point, Charlie interjected, "At least you *got* a present!" Charlie was nursing a grudge because our parents had decided that, starting with this birthday, they were going to abandon the custom of giving the non-birthday child a gift on the other child's birthday. Charlie had complained, "Oh, sure. Just when it's my turn. And besides, she got more years of non-birthday presents than me." He had missed the point that before he'd been born, there had been no non-birthday on which to give me a present.

"No, Charlie," Mom had explained. "We didn't even start doing the double-gift thing until you were one and Lizzie was three. You've had exactly the same number of non-birthday presents."

Charlie had pondered that for a while. I could see the wheels spinning away in there. Finally he'd said in an accusing tone, "Yeah, but she got more presents when she was old enough to care!" My mother, impressed by this flash of logic, stopped arguing. Nevertheless, the custom of non-birthday presents had come to an end.

So, Charlie was put out by my fussing about the socks, and he was whining about my getting another present. "Oh, for crying out loud, Charlie!" I said. "You want a present?

Here!" And I thumped the Sunday socks down by his cereal bowl. "Have these!"

Balancing between irritation and amusement, Mom said, "Oh, c'mon, you two. My gosh." She sighed a theatrical sigh of resignation. "Well, maybe I can find something else in there." She got up and once again rummaged around in the high cupboard. "Aha!"

This time she produced a long, skinny box wrapped in the same cowboy-print paper. Immediately my enthusiasm bubbled back up to its pre-socks level, and I tore open the package. "Hey, this is more like it!"

Encased in the tissue-lined box lay a bright pair of elastic Hopalong Cassidy suspenders with shiny silver clips. I was surprised and pleased. I often wore my older cousin Bill's hand-me-down blue jeans for play, and they had belt loops, so I could just wear a belt to keep the jeans up, but sometimes I wore girls' trousers, and they zipped up the side, or, even less sensibly, in the back. Since even girls' pants were usually too big around for me, and since they often lacked belt loops, I needed something to hold them up.

I wasn't really crazy about the idea of wearing suspenders, but I also didn't enjoy the waistband lumps that resulted when Mom took in my pants and skirts enough to fit my sticklike and hipless figure. The suspender idea had presented itself when Mom had taken Charlie downtown to the boys' department of Samuel's Clothing Store to look for new dressy pants, and I had been taken along. Wandering around the store while Mom threatened and cajoled a reluctant and disgusted Charlie into one pair of pants after another, I had spotted a rack of cowboy suspenders. My first choice would have been Roy Rogers, but they had none of those, so it was either Gene Autry or Hopalong Cassidy, and I much preferred Mr. Cassidy's horse. It was, after all, white, and Gene Autry's horse was brown. Plain brown.

At the time, I had pointed out the suspenders to my mother, but she had pretty much had her hands full trying to be sufficiently firm with Charlie to keep him in line, while at the same time pretending to be calm and pleasant with the young salesman, who was quite annoying. He was one of that syrupy band who affected jolly camaraderie while harboring bored irritation. He kept trying to engage Charlie's good will with comments like, "Say, young fella, you look pretty handsome in those britches. Yes, sir, the young ladies will be after you when you wear those pants down the street." The man had no idea how sadly misdirected his efforts were. The only thing Charlie cared less about than whether he looked good in those britches was whether girls found him irresistible in them.

Given the circumstances, I hadn't thought I'd been very successful directing my mother's attention to the suspender display, so I was pretty surprised to open the box and find Hopalong Cassidy and Topper reclining within. My parents were both grinning over my obvious delight, and Dad said, "Ya know, Mama, I think she likes those even better than the socks."

Mom shook her head and said, "I guess so. Well, maybe I'll get her into ruffles when she's nine!"

CHAPTER FOUR

When breakfast was over, I could tell that the day was going to resume its ordinary rhythm, so I took my new suspenders and my grudgingly tolerated socks upstairs to my bedroom. I dressed myself in my cowboy shirt and hand-me-down jeans, which I thought would constitute an appropriate trial for my suspenders. I managed to get them clipped on to the waistband in front, but I couldn't reach around to hook them in back. I took the jeans off, attached the suspenders in the back and the front, and stepped back into the jeans. This method worked fine, and I now felt snugly anchored within my pants. The full-length mirror was in the hall, so I stepped out to have a look at myself.

My appearance afforded me both plusses and minuses. The jeans, the cowboy shirt, and the new suspenders, I thought, were on the positive side. I was lean as an arrow in the legs and hips, which I thought was the way real cowboys were built, and the suspenders were a positive addition. When I wore a belt, I always had to pull it so tight that my dad said I looked like a bundle of straw tied around the middle. I had no adequate standard by which to assess my face. I just accepted it as it was…a skinny little girl's face, mostly points and angles and big green eyes. I would have been pretty content with the overall picture I presented had it not been for my hair.

Like nearly all mothers in those days, my mom was a devotee of the home permanent. Because I begged her, tearfully, not to give me one, she compromised by applying the curlers "just to the ends." As a result my hair lay shiny and flat from my center part to a point just above my ears, where it blossomed into a frizzy coil that circled my head and formed a puffy, ear-level shelf of tight curls. My mom, who could see that her vision of soft waves had not quite been achieved, assured me that my hair would die down, but until that transpired, I was spending a lot of time with my felt cowboy hat squashed down as low as it would go. This had the effect of flattening most of the wiry little circlets and squeezing the rest out in a rim of frizz just beneath my hat brim. I think my mother was a little depressed at the sight, but she had developed a resilient attitude where I was concerned. Occasionally she would tell me that I had good bone structure, and that when I grew up I would be pretty. This pronouncement was irrelevant to me, but a comfort to her.

After checking the effect of the suspenders in the mirror, and realizing that my lunch present was still hours away, I pulled on my cowboy boots and went down the stairs and out the door in search of my friend Robert.

CHAPTER FIVE

Robert Connor Sherwood was my next-door neighbor and my best friend, and he was soon to   play a pivotal role in the greatest adventure of my life, but neither of us knew that on the morning of my eighth birthday.   Robert was seven years old and a grade behind me, but we had been best friends since he had moved in next door when he was three.   The fact that he was always called "Robert" and not "Bobby" or "Robbie" or any other nickname tells you something about him.   He was not a boy who leant himself to informalities, at least not with most people. He was as tall as I was, but he was so quiet and reserved that he seemed shorter somehow.   He had dark brown hair and enormous dark eyes and perfect features, and even as I child I recognized that he was what adults would consider handsome.

Although Robert was shy and withdrawn around most people, he was different around me.   Robert and I just released something in each other.   If you've ever had a friend like that, you know what I mean.   When Robert and I were together, Robert's protective layer peeled away, and he became, like Pinocchio, a real boy. We played board games and did puzzles and roller-skated down the bumpy sidewalks of Cayuga Street on our rackety metal-wheeled roller skates. We explored the alley behind our houses and played on the playground of South School kitty-corner from my house. We played jacks and marbles and kick-the-can and hide-and-seek. But our best times together, the times that stand out in my memory and make me long with all my heart to be a child again, were the times we spent in the games of our imaginations.

Most of those games took place in our attic, which had much to recommend it as a refuge and a stage set. The most important thing, of course, was that it was far away from the normal haunts of the adults in our world. Robert and I, and sometimes Charlie, would climb to the attic up a steep and narrow back stairway, which, my mother had explained, had once been a servants' stairway. The door leading to those stairs was tucked away in the back of a dark and airless closet, a closet that became an antechamber between a well-lit and ordinary household and a hushed and promising fantasy. There was another set of stairs that led to the attic, but they were commonplace steps that held neither darkness nor mystery, and we rarely chose to use them.

In winter the attic could get pretty cold, especially on cloudy days, so we didn't venture there often. On summer afternoons the still, musty heat rising beneath the rafters made it difficult to breathe, much less play. But in the spring and fall, and on sleepy summer mornings, the attic beckoned.

In the days before everything was disposable, an attic was the repository of a family's history, and by the time I was a child playing in that house on Cayuga Street, the house had been in our family for seventy or eighty years, having been built by my great-grandfather Judge Harper for his bride, Bernadette. A lot of curious and enticing treasures had accumulated up in that aerie in the interim. Just the previous spring we had discovered an old wire-framed dress dummy that scared us to death until we figured out what it was. My cousin Mary (the same cousin who had initiated me into the possibilities of the third-grade girls' restroom) had been leading Robert, Charlie, and me on a tour of exploration behind an old coat rack when the dummy loomed up before us. We were all startled, but Mary, in her nine-year-old wisdom, had explained what it was, and after that it became an object of interest and speculation.

As it happened, there was also an old Civil War sword hanging in its original scabbard from that coat rack. Mary remembered that it had belonged to my great-great-grandfather Emerson on my mother's side of the family. It was Mary who first came up with the idea of spearing the dress dummy. She stood there, fingering the blunt old sword, and suggested the plan in a casual way, as though it made little difference to her one way or another.

"I wonder if it would stick through that old dummy," she said, not looking at us.

Charlie, Robert, and I glanced nervously from one to another. We were clearly out of our depth. It seemed a forbidden and dangerous thing to do. Certainly none of us wanted to go first.

After an uneasy minute or two, Mary leveled the sword at the dummy's midsection and poked it gently through the heavy brittle paper that stretched around the wire frame. There was a satisfying crackling sound when the tip of the sword broke through the paper, leaving an inch-long wound. And there we were, four little sharks who had tasted blood.

Mary gripped the sword in both hands and, backing up five or six feet, she ran straight at the dummy, the sword sticking out in front of her. There was a ripping sound as the sword went clear through the dummy and came out the back. Mary stopped, withdrawing the sword from the frame and wordlessly surveying the damage. She looked over at the three of us standing, round-eyed, in silent awe.

And then we were all grabbing for the sword and hissing, "My turn! My turn!" in fierce whispers. Oddly, we never raised our voices throughout the subsequent destruction. There was just something about the operation...something risky and secret...that seemed to call for subterfuge.

We took turns after that, charging and slicing that old dummy until it was just a ruin of bent wire and shredded paper. Charlie was only five-and-a-half. He could barely lift the sword, but he managed to raise it point-first in the air long enough to let it fall against the dummy, creating a series of gashes along the shoulders. It took the four of us about ten minutes to reduce it to such a state that we could do no further damage, and when we were through we were pretty stunned at what we'd done.

Having made the final charge myself, I stood there, breathing heavily in the warm dusty air, the sword hanging heavily from my hand. It had been my first real act of vandalism, and I felt the weightiness of the moment.

Apprehension was creeping over us. Robert, though, looked frozen. He stared at the shredded dummy and murmured, "What if my dad finds out?"

Mary and I looked at Robert, then at each other. After a minute Mary said, "Don't worry, Robert. If they say anything, we'll tell our parents it was just us three."

"What?" Charlie was outraged. "C'mon. Robert did more'n me!"

"Charlie," I said. "Listen. Robert's dad might be really mad. We'll just say it was you and me and Mary. C'mon, Charlie. Nobody will prob'ly find out anyway."

Charlie looked at me uncertainly, but something in my face or my voice must have impressed him a little. "Well, okay, I guess," he said grudgingly. The adventure had turned pretty sour on him.

We put the sword back in the scabbard, and then we picked up all the loose paper and put it in an old bushel basket. We shoved what was left of the wire frame back into a dark place where the attic turned a corner behind the chimney.

None of our parents ever said anything about it. I guess they never knew. There wasn't much call for a dress dummy in our house in 1953.

CHAPTER SIX

We had stayed away from the attic for a few days after that, playing instead in our living room or in our back yards or down by the lake. We rarely played at Robert's house. It was different over there. First of all, Robert was an only child, so the climate at his house wasn't very childlike. Robert's mom was nice, but she was quiet and shy. When my own mom entered a room, the whole place usually seemed livelier…more awake, more fun. When Robert's mom came into a room, it actually seemed to get quieter. It was an uncomfortable feeling.

Robert's mom was different in other ways, too. She didn't go out very often, and I never saw her sitting at their kitchen table drinking coffee with a friend. She didn't even drive their car…she didn't know how. Charlie and I found that baffling. It seemed almost to exclude her from the adult world.

She was always nice to me, and to Charlie, when he was along, but our presence seemed to make her uneasy. When

Robert's dad was home, her uneasiness acquired a sharper edge, as though she were responsible not only for her own behavior, but for ours as well.

Robert's house held little allure in the form of playthings, either. Robert's little blue-wallpapered room was always so neat and clean that it seemed like nobody lived there, least of all a child. Robert didn't have very many toys, and the ones he did have were arranged in perfect rows on the shelf by his bed.

He had a baseball glove, which he rarely used. He had some marbles in a cigar box, and he had one of the smaller Erector sets. He played with the Erector set sometimes, but he wasn't allowed to leave any of the structures up when he was done playing, so he lost interest after a while.

What Robert did have were books. My mother told me that Mrs. Sherwood bought them for him with her grocery money. Robert kept a few books on his toy shelf, but most of them were stored under his bed or stacked neatly on the floor of his closet. Robert's dad thought books were for sissies, but he rarely came into Robert's bedroom, and he never looked under the bed or in the closet.

One Friday afternoon, when Robert and I had been in his room looking at his pirate book, his mom had come hurrying in. "Guess what, Robert! Daddy's home early! Let's just put these books away for now. We'll get everything all tidy for Daddy!"

She had given us a big smile, but kids know when a smile is stretched too tight. When the books were put away, and his mom had left the room, I looked a question at my friend, but he just shrugged and said, "My dad likes things neat. It's just easier this way."

It always seemed odd to me that Robert would hide his books, because he was crazy about reading. He read with an almost fierce sort of concentration. When he got involved in a book, it was as though a bubble formed around him. Sometimes, in order to get his attention, I'd have to put my head down between his face and the book. "Robert," I'd say, "You have to go home now. It's supper time."

His eyes would slowly refocus on my face, inches from his own, and then a slow grin would play around his mouth. "It's supper time already?"

Robert read books on everything. He read fiction books about detectives and cowboys and explorers and ordinary people. He read the Dr. Dolittle books and the Marguerite Henry books and the Hardy Boys books. He read biographies, which no children read, and he read non-fiction books about wars and dinosaurs and rockets and animals. He read just about everything, and it seemed like he never forgot anything.

My mother told me that Robert had learned to read when he was three, and one of the first books he ever read was a big picture book about horses that belonged to my cousin

Mary. She was six at the time, and, like so many young girls, had developed a fascination with horses. Her picture book illustrated all the breeds of horses and all the gear that went with them. Mary had forgotten the book at our house, and Robert had come across it. Mom said that he sat down and puzzled over that book for a long time, figuring out most of the words for himself and asking Mom about some of the hard ones.

Three years later, when Robert was six and I was seven, we were playing cowboy one day in the living room and decided to make a horse out of the piano bench, using a folded-up afghan for a saddle. Robert said, "We can use a belt for the girth."

"What's a girth?" I asked.

"Oh, it's that strap that holds the saddle on."

"How do you know?"

"Oh, it was in that book of Mary's, the one with all the horse pictures in it."

My mom came out of the kitchen, wiping her hands on a dishtowel. She was looking at Robert with a quizzical little smile on her face. "Robert, do you really remember that book?"

Robert looked off into space for a moment and said, "Oh, yeah, it had a picture of a palomino...like Roy Rogers' horse...on the cover, and it had a chart of all the kinds of horses, and it had a picture of a saddle with all the parts named. I remember 'girth' and 'pommel' and 'stirrup.' Oh, and 'horn'."

Mom shook her head and said, "Wow." That's when she realized just what kind of a memory Robert had. Not wanting to make too big a deal out of it, she had said to me later, "That little friend of yours is pretty smart, isn't he!"

Her comment had surprised me. To me, Robert was Robert. I suppose I considered his unusual fund of knowledge just another of his quirky personality traits.

At any rate, Robert spent a lot of time immersed in his books (and my books, for that matter). But Robert was careful about reading at his own house when his father was home. When Mr. Sherwood was in the house, it was as though Robert was always watching out for something, or listening for something. I didn't know what it was, but it made me feel like I'd better be watching out or listening too.

I knew I wasn't quite comfortable around Robert's parents when they were together. There was something about the way they interacted that made me uneasy. I couldn't put my finger on it exactly, but one day when I met old Collin McGee out with his dog Lazarus, I suddenly recognized the same uneasy feeling. Collin McGee was the only man I'd ever heard my parents label as mean. Both my parents were careful not to make any disparaging remarks about other people in the presence of my brother and me, probably because they didn't want their opinions broadcast, but I had heard my father call Collin McGee a "mean old son-of-a-gun" on more than one occasion. My mother warned Charlie and me to stay away from his house.

Mr. McGee lived alone, which was no surprise, but he had a little terrier named Lazarus who, in the way of all dogs, just worshiped old Collin without reservation, never receiving anything for all his adoration but kicks and curses. Old Mr. McGee lived across the street and two doors down from our house. Every morning he would appear, scratching and yawning, at his front door, dressed in his pajama pants and undershirt. He'd open the screen and little Lazarus would scoot out, slinking and scurrying, to pick up the newspaper from the front walk. He'd get the paper in his mouth and scuttle back to the front door, keeping himself low to the sidewalk. When he reached the door he'd hunker down on his belly and peek up at Mr. McGee, but all his master ever said was, "You stupid mutt." Then he'd open the screen again and Lazarus would get halfway up and skitter sideways through the door, wary of a welcoming kick on the way in.

Of course, I'd never seen Robert's dad treat his mom like that, and, in fact, when he was around me he was usually pretty quiet. When he was out in the yard and my parents were around, he was actually kind of jovial and friendly. So I wasn't quite sure why the sight of Lazarus should bring Robert's mom to my mind. When Charlie and I were over at Robert's house, she was always smiling and kind and thoughtful, but there was also something else...something hesitant and anxious...that made it hard to relax in her presence.

There was one other incident involving Robert's parents that added to my occasional feeling of unease, and it was something I'd overheard way back on an evening the previous August. I'd been in bed for perhaps an hour, Charlie had been sound asleep, and I'd found myself lying awake, hot and uncomfortable, and feeling like I might like a drink of cold water and a little company. I'd gotten out of bed and started down the stairs, drawn by the drone of my parents' conversation in the living room below. When I reached the lower landing their dialogue came into focus and I heard the word "Robert." For some reason, that gave me pause, and I stopped to listen.

"Well, I do worry about him. No six-year-old should have to live with that."

Dad's half-attentive voice responded, "Oh, if it's that bad, she could just leave."

"Oh, Bob, be realistic. Where would she go? She doesn't have a dime."

"Doesn't she have a sister in Denver or somewhere?"

"Yes, but you know Inez. She'd never be willing to be a burden."

"She could get a job."

"I can't see Paul letting his wife get a job. He doesn't even let her drive."

"Well, it's none of our business. I don't see what we can do." My dad's voice carried that hint of irritation that signaled the end of a conversation, but he added, almost to himself, "He had a rough time in North Africa. He was pretty easy-going when I knew him back in high school."

At that point I'd heard my mom get up from her chair saying, "Want some lemonade?" I'd risen from the landing and scurried back to bed, my head full of disturbing images. Mr. Sherwood had been in Africa? Why? I didn't know my dad had known him in high school, either. And why would Mrs. Sherwood want to go to Denver? Why was my mom worried about Robert? I wanted to ask my parents all these questions, but I knew I had not been meant to overhear, so I was reluctant to admit eavesdropping. I crept quietly back to my bed, more wide awake than ever, and lay there, my mind filled with dark and troublesome thoughts. It took me a long time to go to sleep, but the morning brought a flood of sunlight and a summer's day, and I forgot all about the worrisome conversation. I had adjusted to the fact that we rarely played over at Robert's, and that he sometimes couldn't come over on weekends, and that was just the way it was.

CHAPTER SEVEN

And so, on the Friday morning of my eighth birthday, I went over to Robert's, knocked on the back screen, and, when he appeared, asked, "Can you come out?"

Robert looked back over his shoulder and then, turning to me, said, "I'm not sure. My dad's home early for the weekend."

Robert's dad was a traveling salesman. He drove from one little Iowa town to the next, selling cheap little toys and knick-knacks and funny gadgets to drug stores and gift shops and gas stations. He usually came home on Wednesday nights and weekends. When his dad was home, Robert was especially careful to be well-behaved, even though the rules of behavior often seemed ill defined.

"Ask your mom, why don't you?" I advised.

Robert paused, one hand holding the screen door open while he looked vaguely back into the kitchen.

"Okay," he finally said, and he let the door bang before disappearing into his living room. I could hear him talking to his mom.

"Mom, Lizzie's here. Can I go out and play? It's her birthday."

His mom's voice, full of hesitation, answered, "Oh, I don't know, Robert. You're going to the show with her this afternoon, you know. Maybe you should stay in and help around the house a little this morning."

Then I heard his dad's voice. "Oh, for Chrissake, Inez. Let the kid get some exercise. He hangs around here like a little spook."

"Oh, well then, go ahead, Robert." His mom's voice was edged with a nervous brightness. "Come home for lunch."

Robert reappeared in the kitchen, and looming up behind him was his father. "So, here's our big birthday girl!" Mr. Sherwood's greeting was full of hearty cheer. He often sounded that way when he talked to me or my family or any of the neighbors.

Knowing enough not to irritate him, I replied, "Yup! I'm eight!" I looked up at him and grinned, hoping to ease Robert's transition from his house.

Robert slid quickly out the screen door, and together we hopped self-consciously down his back porch steps. Mr. Sherwood stood in the doorway and watched us. We hurried around the side of the house, out of sight of the back door.

Dimly aware of some lingering tension, I blurted, "Your dad's home early."

"Yeah. He got home last night. He said he needed a long weekend." Something guarded in Robert's voice told me he wasn't looking forward to having his dad home for three days, so I changed the subject.

"Whadda you wanna do?"

"I dunno. Whadda you wanna play?"

"I asked you first."

"Well, I don't care."

"Let's be Hillary and Tenzing."

"Okay. Dibs on Hillary."

Robert and I were enthralled with the mountain-climbing feat of Edmund Hillary and his Sherpa, Tenzing, which had taken place the previous May. We'd been playing mountain climber ever since, using the Indian trails or the boxes piled in our attic as Mount Everest.

Robert looked back at his kitchen window for a minute. Then he said, "I can't go to the lake unless I ask my mom."

He and I knew it would be risky to initiate another encounter with his father, so I suggested, "Okay. Let's just play in the attic."

We climbed my front porch steps and met my brother Charlie coming out the front door. Charlie was wearing his favorite item of clothing, a long-sleeved, white cotton shirt that buttoned down the front. He had been wearing the same shirt about twice a week for a year. It was so worn out from washing and wearing that it was almost transparent, and the cuffs and collar were frayed to the point of fluffiness.

Charlie's fondness for this or any other garment was a mystery to the family. When asked about it, Charlie shrugged and replied, "I just like it. It doesn't stick to my skin."

In our childhood circle of acquaintances, Charlie and I knew dozens of brother-sister combinations, and it had occurred to me that I liked my little brother better than most sisters liked their brothers. Part of it may have been his quirkiness, which made him interesting. Part of it was no doubt the low-key nonchalance that characterized his relationships. Like most younger siblings, he wanted to be included, but Charlie was different in that he wasn't desperate about it, and he was usually willing to be assigned supporting roles.

"Whatcha doin'?" he asked that morning, wheeling around and following us back through the front door. "Whereya goin', you guys?"

Robert and I headed up the steps with Charlie clambering up after us. Every few steps he repeated, "Whereya goin'?"

Since Charlie was my brother, not Robert's, I felt free to ignore him for longer stretches of time. Finally, Robert responded, "We're goin' to the attic."

Charlie persisted, "Whatcha gonna play?"

I assumed my leadership position and said, "We're playing mountain climber, and only Hillary and Tenzing made it to the top, so if you wanna play, you have to stay back at the base camp."

"What's a base camp?" Charlie asked.

I drew on my store of information obtained from the newspaper articles about the expedition—articles that Robert and I had devoured and memorized. "It's a camp lower down the mountain where they leave all their extra stuff. And the climbers who are just helpers have to stay there."

Charlie stopped on the top step, considering his options. Though not offended by his relegation to a supporting role, he was weighing the potential for fun if he were restricted to a lower stack of boxes while Charlie and I climbed to the top of the orange crates, leaning heavily on our yardsticks and struggling for oxygen. Then he gave a little shrug and followed us down the hall. He was a practical person and probably would have been content in real life to stay back at the base camp, digging through the supplies for snacks while the summit team battled through an ice storm on its way to the top.

The three of us passed through the little closet leading to the attic stairway, a narrow, dim passage lit only by the sunlight filtering in from the circle of stained glass set into the eastern wall at the top of the stairs. Seventy years earlier, when a teen-aged servant girl had slept up there, the light from that window must have provided a little solace in the otherwise drab loneliness of an attic bedroom.

We always paused when we came to the window to peek out through the little octagon of clear glass in the center. Off to the left was the St. Mary's church, and across the alley was the big brick house where the Andersons lived, with Nathan Samuels' house next to it. Looking off to the right, we could see quite a ways down the alley behind our house. The alley bordered everyone's back yard, and back yards contained the endless summer possibilities of vegetable gardens, storage sheds, and kids' outdoor toys. We could see the back few feet of Mrs. Krebb's strawberry patch...a sight that triggered the memory of one of the few real humiliations in my life up to that point.

It had taken place two years earlier when I was six, my cousin Mary was eight, and my cousin Bill was eleven. The three of us had found ourselves bored and restless on a Sunday afternoon after a big family dinner at our house. The adults were sitting in the living room chatting and, in some cases, snoozing. The older girl cousins, Judy and Sue, (older sisters of Mary and Bill, respectively) had retreated to the front porch where they could be teenagers in peace. Charlie and our four-year-old cousin Jim (Bill's little brother) were occupied upstairs with Charlie's toy cars and trucks. The Armstrong cousins had been taken home so the littlest of the eight kids (Dad's sister had married a Catholic) could be put down for naps.

Bill and Mary went out the back door, and I tagged along behind. We wandered lazily down the alley, kicking up the dust with our stiff and shiny Sunday shoes. As we approached Mrs. Krebb's abundant patch of strawberries, I noticed Bill and Mary exchanging glances and grinning conspiratorially. A few seconds later, they dropped to their hands and knees and crawled down behind the staked tomato plants lining the edge of the strawberry bed. Staying low, they hunkered along the outside row of strawberry plants, picking fast and eating as they went.

For a minute, I stood in the alley and watched them in bewilderment. After a bit, I stepped to the back of the patch, carefully selected a fat berry or two, and ate them slowly, without subtlety or guilt.

Mary hissed at me, "Lizzie, scrunch down! She'll see you!"

I was confused. The fact was, Mrs. Krebb appeared at our front door every other day, bringing little containers of berries and other produce from her garden to share with my family. Weren't these the same berries?

Mary was gesturing frantically now. "Get down. Geez, here she comes!" Her warning was punctuated by the banging of a screen door as Mrs. Krebb emerged, red-faced and tight-lipped, and tramped angrily down her garden path in my direction.

With a ripe berry halfway to my mouth, I watched her in surprise and consternation, then turned to ask Mary what to do, but Mary and Bill were disappearing around the side of the Hibbs' storage shed. I could hear them, suppressing laughter and urging each other to hurry as they threw themselves into hiding places in the weeds.

Turning back to face Mrs. Krebb, I was met with the sight of a woman I had only known as kindly and generous, now turned accusatory and frightening. She shook her finger at me and scolded, "Lizzie, don't you know that's stealing? Those are *not* your berries! You should know better! Shame on you! What would your mother say?"

I stood there a minute in my Sunday dress, hot with humiliation and injured pride. The injustice of Mrs. Krebb's tirade and my cousins' betrayal slowly sank in, and I burst into angry tears. I turned and walked back down the alley, crying miserably and wiping my face with the backs of my hands. When I passed the shed, Mary and Bill slipped out of their hiding places and joined me, looking back over their shoulders to make sure Mrs. Krebb hadn't decided to follow me home to tell my mom.

Walking along on either side of me, they flapped their arms and admonished me. "Lizzie, why didn't you *run*? You just *stood* there!" The whole incident left me shaken and confused and mad. Why would Mrs. Krebb be so stingy about a few berries removed from her patch when she was so generous about removing them and sharing them herself? It seemed to me we'd saved her the trouble of picking. Did she just want the credit? The next time she came to babysit for us, she acted as thought the whole incident had never taken place. Perhaps she'd forgotten it, but I hadn't. And I was reminded of it every time I went by her back yard.

CHAPTER EIGHT

The day of my birthday, however, Robert was more concerned with what he could see of his own house across the way. "I can see my bedroom window," said Robert, pressing his cheek to the colored panes so he could see sideways out the peek hole. "I can see my back door and the kitchen window and...our garage and...and the door to the coal chute."

Meanwhile, Charlie had turned his attention to the stacks of boxes and orange crates along the attic walls. "Where's Mount Everest?" he asked, surveying the scene for the highest ground.

I pointed to a graduated pile of crates, boxes, and wardrobe trunks. "Over there." And just in case he'd forgotten his assigned post, I indicated a lower pile under the angle of the rafters and added, "That's base camp."

I started towards the orange crate mountain, stepping over a fishing tackle box and an old picnic basket. Then, as I put my foot down on a stack of old Life magazines, an odd thing happened. The magazine on the top of the pile slipped a little under my weight and, as I leaned quickly forward to keep my balance, the magazine flew out from under me. I put the other foot down to keep my balance, and the next issue, propelled backward by my attempt to stay upright, shot out behind as well. Still trying not to fall I continued to alternate feet, and fwap! fwap! fwap! Six, seven, eight Life magazines went flying. Charlie and Robert stood spellbound.

When I did finally lose my balance, I crashed forward onto my hands and knees in a jarring fall that left me momentarily speechless. Charlie and Robert leapt forward, unconcerned about my fall.

"Wow! That was neat! Did you do that on purpose? How did you do that? Can I try?" They were gathering up the scattered magazines, restacking them, lining up the corners and patting them down.

I pulled myself up, and the three of us spent the next fifteen minutes trying every way we could come up with to reproduce my experience. All we got for our efforts were banged shins and badly damaged magazines. Finally Robert sat down on an empty refrigerator crate and said philosophically, "It's no use. Some things have to be by accident." He paused, and then added an afterthought. "There's good accidents and bad accidents. They're nobody's fault. This was a good accident." He paused. "Good accidents aren't as common as bad accidents." Robert talked that way sometimes, but everyone ignored him.

By that time, we agreed that the mountain-climbing mood had somehow passed. "Well, what should we do then?" asked Charlie.

I shrugged. "I wonder what time it is." I was thinking about what the rest of the day held in store. One more present was due at lunch, and after lunch, it would be almost time to leave for the movie, which was Walt Disney's *Peter Pan*. Robert and I had been anticipating that movie for months. We'd seen the previews, and Robert had been so enthralled he'd actually read the original book by J. M. Barrie. He told me not to bother. He said that either it wasn't written for kids, or else it was written for kids a long time ago, and they must have talked differently then. Even so, he knew the story well.

The Orpheum Theater must have been expecting record crowds, because the movie was to be shown on Friday afternoon and evening as well as on Saturday and Sunday. I'd told my mom that we would need to get there early. I didn't want to take any chances, and I didn't want to get stuck in the front row and have to watch the whole thing with my neck craned up to see the screen.

Robert's thoughts had also drifted to the movie we were both so eager to see. He was looking thoughtfully up at the jumble of crates and boxes. "I know," he said. "Let's take down Mount Everest and build Neverland!" All three of us were captivated with Robert's idea. Now that we had a goal, we were seized with energy. For the next two hours we immersed ourselves in the creation of our island. We built the Lost Boys' underground tree hideout from orange crates and Mermaid Lagoon from army blankets draped over sawhorses. We made an Indian camp with a teepee of Christmas tablecloths hung from the coat rack. The biggest challenge, and the greatest success, was our pirate ship.

There was a big wooden refrigerator crate in the attic. It must have been almost impossible to carry it up two flights of stairs and around corners, but someone, probably my frugal mom, must have deemed it worth saving, because there it was. We turned it on its side and the side that was now the top swung open and lay down flat next to the adjoining edge of the box. Now it was like a big bathtub. We put up a broom handle mast, and we arranged an assortment of smaller boxes inside the crate, knowing that we'd want to have our swordfights on more than one level. There was a plank for "walking the plank," but we couldn't figure out how to anchor it well enough on one end, so our plank was actually more of a bridge from the edge of our refrigerator crate over to the top of an army trunk. We just jumped off in the middle of the plank, pretending we'd come to the end.

When we were looking for cardboard mailing tubes to use as cannons, we came across a bushel basket of Christmas lights. We untangled them and strung them along the edges of the crate, up the mast, and along the plank. We dug around in a box of old tools until we found a filthy old extension cord, which we used to connect the Christmas lights into the single electrical outlet in the far attic wall. Charlie and Robert stood respectfully back while I plugged in the cord. The pirate ship sprang to life. Even in the soft daylight filtering through the stained glass window, the colored lights stood out, defining an enchanted ship. Surrounded by the lagoon, the Indian camp, and the tree house, Captain Hook's ship was now the centerpiece of our Neverland. Charlie, Robert, and I climbed in and basked in the glow, a little awed by what we had created. We sat for a few moments, not speaking, each of us transported to a kingdom where children without parents were free to fight pirates, consort with Indians, and go to bed when they felt like it.

By then the attic was getting pretty warm, and we knew it must be pretty close to lunchtime. I saw Robert give a little start as he realized suddenly how late it must be. He climbed out of the crate and picked his way over to the attic window. Peering down through the peek hole in the stained glass, he said, "I can see my mom in the kitchen. I think she's fixing lunch. I better go. I really wanna see *Peter Pan.*"

I nodded in support. Robert's dad often grounded his son for unpredictable reasons. There was no point in taking any chances. "It starts at two," I said. "Come on over early."

"If I can," Robert called back from halfway down the attic stairs. Charlie and I sat there for a few minutes more, but Robert's departure had broken the mood, and we realized we were hungry. I unplugged the Christmas lights, and we tramped down the two flights to the kitchen, where Mom was fussing over the stove. I could smell the cheesy aroma of macaroni and cheese.

CHAPTER NINE

Now that lunchtime had arrived, I was pretty curious to see what my midday gift would be. In keeping with the save-the-best-for-last protocol, I was pretty certain that the lunch present would be better than the suspenders, but not as good as my anticipated knife. A book, maybe. Or a pinball game.

I sat down at the kitchen table. Charlie was sitting under the table, playing with Edmund Hillary, who was at that time somewhere between a kitten and a cat. Even my parents had capitulated to the charms of Edmund Hillary. He was haughty and lovable by turns. He appeared always to be in deep and inscrutable thought. He liked catching crickets but was disdainful of mouse hunting. He was lean and gangly and very acrobatic. My whole family was impressed by his ability to spring, pogo-stick-like, straight up into the air without a running start. Still, he was a cat, and by my mother's standards, he was not quite clean.

"Okay, Charlieboy, wash your hands for lunch."

"My hands aren't dirty," Charlie answered, examining his palms.

"You've been playing with the cat."

"But Edmund Hillary's really clean, Mom. He washes himself about six hours a day."

My dad walked in from the back porch and, having overheard the last two or three comments, said, "Wash your hands, Charlie."

"Oh, for crying out loud! All right!"

Lunch consisted of macaroni and cheese, apple slices, and chocolate chip cookies (all my favorites) in honor of my birthday. Charlie was fond of the menu as well, but he ate lunch even more slowly than he ate breakfast. Without a cereal box to read, he sometimes just stopped in the middle of a bite, staring into space and forgetting to chew until Mom thwacked him on the cheek with her finger. I wasn't looking forward to waiting for Charlie to come out of his trance long enough to get a plateful of macaroni down.

I offered a suggestion. "Hey, maybe I could have my lunch present *before* lunch!"

Mom paused for a second, holding a plate of macaroni in each hand. She was thinking it over, which I took to be a promising sign.

"Ummmm, I don't think so."

"Why not?"

"One, lunch is ready. And two, if you open this present, you won't want to eat. You'll want to play."

"Really?"

"I'm pretty sure."

Now I was even more eager for lunch to be over. "Okay, but Charlie has to keep chewing."

I gulped down my lunch as fast as I could. Charlie tried to eat at his usual speed, but every time I saw his jaw winding down, I flapped my arms at him and encouraged, "Chew, Charlie, chew!" He rolled his eyes, but he kept chewing.

After lunch, my mom cleared away the dishes, and while I fidgeted in anticipation, my dad stood up and glanced thoughtfully around the room as though looking for something he'd mislaid.

He mused, "Ya know, it seems like I saw a box in here earlier. Quite a big box actually. Wonder where it went."

"C'mon, Dad! It's my present! Where is it?"

My father was enjoying himself. He looked all over the kitchen, even gazing speculatively into the garage can. He wandered absentmindedly out onto the back porch, letting the screen door bang shut behind him. There were three more bangs as I, then Charlie, then Mom followed him out. Dad looked distractedly around the back yard, then peered towards the garage, arching one eyebrow and murmuring, "Hmmm, ya know, I think maybe...."

I was dancing around him like a crazed moon orbiting a slow-moving planet. We all trailed after him into our stuffy one-car garage, and there in the middle of the cement floor was a big cardboard box with the words "Sears and Roebuck" on the side.

"It's my gas station!" I was elated. I knew instantly what was inside the box, because our local Sears and Roebuck store didn't offer many toys, and the only one I had recently admired was this model gas station. It had a little elevator that went up and down, a ramp for the cars, a tiny gasoline pump and rubber hose, and little cars and miniature people.

I jumped up and down and raised a ruckus while my dad grinned and my mom half-smiled and shook her head. Charlie and I tried to tear into the box, but it was held shut by fat metal staples that my dad had to remove with a screwdriver. The gas station itself required some assembly, so Charlie and I were again required to wait while my father put it together, folding back all the little metal tabs and flattening them with a block of wood. When it was finally set up, we carried it into the living room and put it on a card table. By then it was nearly time to leave for the movie.

I was feeling pretty good about the gas station. It was, I knew, moderately expensive. I thought I remembered a five-dollar sticker on the store model. And yet it wasn't so expensive as to preclude my chances for a pricier gift like a hunting knife, which cost a little over six dollars, including the sheath. It was the perfect middle present. My birthday, I thought, was turning out great.

CHAPTER TEN

At that point, Mom announced that it was time for Charlie and me to go up and wash our hands and faces before the movie. As we headed for the stairs, I said, mostly to myself, "I sure hope Robert can go. His dad's home."

Mom was gathering her purse and car keys, but she stopped and said, "Oh, that's right. Paul's home, isn't he."

"Yeah, he came home a day early this week."

Our mother stood there a moment, looking thoughtfully at us and tossing her keys gently in one hand. Then she got a determined little smile on her face and said brightly, "Tell you what. You kids get washed up, and I'll go over and pick Robert up myself."

My dad, who was standing a few feet away, was smiling oddly and muttering something about Mr. Sherwood being out of luck. I hoped that meant that Robert would be going with us. Mom went out the front door and down the steps. Charlie and I looked at each other and raised our eyebrows.

Charlie nodded and said, "Mr. Sherwood won't say no to Mom. He's always nice to grown-ups."

"Yeah, he is," I agreed, but I was surprised Charlie had noticed. You never knew with Charlie.

We ran upstairs to clean up. Before we went back downstairs, Charlie slipped into our room and took two dimes out of the cigar box he used for a bank. Our parents always gave us enough money for one treat, but Charlie liked his candy supply to last through the film, and he never took chances. I usually managed to make one box of Jujifruits last the whole movie, and Robert always bought popcorn. I found out years later that Mom always supplied Robert with treat money. He only had enough to pay for his ticket.

We bounded down the stairs and out onto the porch. I was relieved to see Mom and Robert coming down the driveway toward us. Robert was holding Mom's hand and looking down at the ground as he walked. Behind them, Mr. Sherwood stood on his back porch. His face was expressionless as he watched his son's departure. Mom seemed oblivious to any tension. She smiled easily and sang out, "Okay, who's ready for the movies?"

We ran down the front steps and out to the curb where our Ford station wagon was parked. Robert and Charlie and I scrambled into the back seat. We preferred the back seat, as it was farthest from the driver and seemed less vulnerable to adult supervision than the middle seat.

The Orpheum Theater was only about seven blocks from our house. We drove past the high school, the junior high, four churches, the telephone office, the DX station, the depot, and two blocks of stores, and we were there. We piled out of the car. Mom looked over the back of the seat and called out to our departing backs, "Have fun! See you at three-thirty!"

We gave her our absent-minded waves of dismissal as we jockeyed for position in the undulating ticket line. A long, wiggly row of excited kids wound its way through the jumble of bicycles leaning on kickstands or tossed carelessly on the sidewalk. Three or four dogs lay forlornly beside their owners' bikes and gazed worriedly in the direction of the theater doors. Bigger boys of nine or ten shoved and bossed and made themselves obnoxious, undaunted by the irritated protests of "Hey, no cutting in line!"

When we reached the ticket window, Robert paid for his own ticket and I paid for Charlie and myself, since Charlie could barely see above the ticket counter. I knew Charlie's pride was a little wounded, so I tried to reassure him by telling him that it saved time for me to buy both tickets. He probably saw through that, but he shrugged it off, knowing he would assume command again at the candy counter, which was glass most of the way to the floor. Charlie enjoyed special status there anyway, because Erin, the girl at the candy counter, actually knew him by name. Charlie was one of the few kids who came out during the movie to buy more candy.

We bought our treats and pushed through the outer lobby. Between the lobby and the inside of the theater there was a wide, high-ceilinged, curving hallway...a grand entrance that took us from the bright, hard edges of the real world into the wide darkness of the theater, permeated with the smells of popcorn and candy and crowds of kids. The rows of seats rose gradually at first and then sloped more steeply up to the back, where they stopped just below the projectionist's little windows.

The last few rows were unofficially saved for the young teen-agers who gathered there, sometimes pairing off. My cousin Mary had told me that there was a lot of gossip about naughty things that went on in those back rows, but I found it hard to credit. There was a zealous usher named Monroe who, armed with a flashlight and a beleaguered attitude, patrolled the aisles of the Orpheum. He seemed like an old man to us, but he was probably only about forty. Monroe had not had an easy life, and the Orpheum Theater had become his kingdom—a kingdom he ruled with vigilance and little tolerance for shenanigans. Monroe had a noticeable speech problem, and that, combined with his habit of policing the dark rows of the theater, made him an object of derision. He roamed the aisles constantly, shining his flashlight into kids' faces and hissing, "You kidth be quiet!

Thit down and thtop fooling around!" His favorite target was the rear of the theater, up where the teen-agers whispered and giggled and smirked disrespectfully. Monroe was an unyielding force for decorum and morality, which made me skeptical that kids in the back rows were getting away with much.

Robert and Charlie and I always sat about two-thirds of the way back, a few rows up in the steep part, so we could see over the heads of the bigger kids. We found our seats and sat talking and eating and looking around for kids we knew. Everyone else was doing the same thing, and there was an excited buzz of anticipation while we waited for the movie. Seats banged up and down, and a few pieces of popcorn flew through the air. Finally the lights went down, the heavy gold curtains drew back, and "News of the Day" came on in black and white. The crowd bounced and chattered its way through the news, and then sent up a cheer when the "Tom and Jerry" cartoon started. The cartoon was always followed by a few ads for local businesses…Anderson Motors, Angie's Bakery, Heartland Plumbing, and a few others. During the ads a few kids always went tearing out to the restrooms, experience having taught them that they couldn't otherwise make it through a large Coke and the feature film.

When all the preliminaries drew to a close, I felt a Christmas-morning tingle of pleasure. I glanced at Robert, who gave me a little grin. We settled back, secure in our shared anticipation. The story began in London, in the Darling family's home, and from the first glimpse of Wendy, John, and Michael cavorting in their imaginary games while their parents prepared for an evening out, Robert and I were transported. When Peter Pan, near the end of the film, shouted for Tinker Bell to pixie dust the ship, and Captain Hook's pirate ship was transformed into a gleaming, golden vessel lifting into the sky over Neverland, I was so swept up that tears sprang to my eyes. Embarrassed, I hastily brushed them away and glanced nervously to see if Robert had noticed, but he was as captivated as I was, and his wide dark eyes were riveted on the screen.

At the end of the movie, Robert and I sat silently for a moment, reluctantly letting Peter Pan's imaginary world slip away. Around us, kids were bounding from their seats and pushing their way down the crowded aisles. Charlie, who never left the real world very far behind, sat there tolerantly for a minute or so, but then said, "C'mon, you guys! Mom will be waiting!"

Robert and I exchanged a secret, awkward smile. I knew Robert had loved the movie as much as I had. We both knew we'd be acting out its stories for weeks to come, developing new subplots and embellishing every character. Our hearts were already up in our attic Neverland, crossing swords and rescuing each other from Hook.

We went down the steps and out the curving hallway, jostling around with the departing crowd. It was always a little startling when we emerged from the darkened theater to discover the sunlight filling the lobby and reflecting off the diamonds in the broad white sidewalk. Outside, kids were scattering on foot and on bicycles, the three or four dogs overjoyed to be reunited with their owners. Other kids were clambering into the back seats of cars, already excitedly retelling the story of Peter Pan to their moms.

Our own mother was double-parked about four cars back. We ran to the station wagon and flung ourselves into the rear seat. I was slipping away from the spell of Peter Pan and starting to refocus on the remainder of my birthday. The day had gone so well already that it was almost hard to believe that more good things were in store, but I knew what the schedule dictated. The thought of my new knife flitted across my mind, and I visualized how it would fit into our reenactments of Peter's adventures.

"How long til supper? Are we going out? Can Robert go? Can I have my last present before supper?" Robert was looking at me oddly. I think he was a little surprised at and mildly disapproving of such a blatant display of unabashed greed on my part. I really was pretty annoying at that point.

CHAPTER ELEVEN

Had I given it any thought, I would have remembered Robert's last birthday the previous April. His father had given him a baseball glove, but it had come with a price. On the afternoon of his birthday, Robert and his dad had come out into the back yard to play catch. My parents and I had watched them from our kitchen window. I could tell that Robert was nervous, because he kept dropping the ball. When he played with my dad and Charlie and me, he was pretty good. Maybe he just wasn't used to the new glove. Whatever it was, when he played with his father that day, he was awkward and stiff, and he looked pretty miserable.

After about fifteen minutes, Mr. Sherwood shook his head and said, "Okay, Rob, we'll try again when you feel like putting some effort into it." Then he turned and walked back into his house, letting the screen door slam shut behind him.

Robert stood there, staring at the door, then looking at the ground. He punched his fist idly into his glove a few times, then dropped his arms to his sides. The glove slid off his hand and fell to the grass. He stood there a little while longer, and then he picked up the ball and the glove and went in the house. He didn't let the screen door bang. Instead he turned back and closed it slowly, with no sound.

I watched Robert disappear into his house, then looked at my mom and dad. My mother's eyes were glistening, and my father looked solemn. We sat down at the kitchen table, and I wondered what to do. After a quiet minute, I asked, "Should I go over and ask if Robert can play?"

My mom pressed her hands briefly to her eyes and said, "No, Honey, I think Robert probably wants to be alone just now. You can go over later."

My dad sighed, rose from the table, and walked into the living room to his big easy chair. He sat down and picked up the paper and shook it open. Feeling sad and helpless, I sat down on the floor at my father's elbow. He put his hand on my head and ruffled my hair. "I'm glad Robert has you for a friend, Lizzie," he said.

But that day in our station wagon I wasn't thinking about Robert's birthday or Robert's dad. I was thinking about my own birthday and looking forward to the prospect of my knife, which I assumed would be presented at dinner. Unable to contain myself, I was badgering my mom with questions. "Can Robert go out to eat with us? Are you bringing my present to the restaurant? Can I open it there? What about the cake?"

Mom was a little exasperated by the time we pulled into our driveway. She had answered all my questions with a sing-song, "We'll see," but as she was parking the car, we saw Mr. Sherwood over in his own drive, bending over his lawn mower, a screw driver in his hand. He looked hot, and when he spotted us he stood up and mopped at his face with his sleeve.

Mom hitched the strap of her purse up over her shoulder, and I saw a look of resolve come over her face. She said, "There's Paul now. I'll just run over to make sure it's okay for Robert to have dinner with us." There was determination in her voice, reminding me of the time when she had announced, "I'll just fix the darn vacuum cleaner myself." And she had fixed it.

Robert watched Mom walk off towards his father. He looked as though he wanted to stop her but didn't know how. He called, "Wait...maybe...I don't...," but he wasn't very loud, and he couldn't gather his thoughts fast enough to come up with a coherent request.

My mother just strode breezily up to Mr. Sherwood, and in a friendly, nonchalant way, said, "Hi, Paul! Can we borrow Robert for Lizzie's birthday dinner tonight? Lizzie won't have near as much fun with just her own brother!"

Charlie glanced at me indignantly but said nothing. Robert and I were listening intently to what his father might say. Mr. Sherwood was on the spot. I was pretty certain that he wanted to say no, but Mom had phrased her request to make it sound like he would be doing us a personal favor by loaning us his son for the evening. Mr. Sherwood cared how people in the neighborhood thought of him. Finally he said, "Well, we can't disappoint the birthday girl! But send him home right after supper. He's been putting his chores off all day."

He tried to share a conspiratorial grin with my mother, but she'd already turned her back on him. "Great! Now we've got us a real party!" she announced, loud enough for Robert to hear. Robert smiled weakly, but he continued to watch his father, probably expecting him to change his mind. My mother must have considered that possibility as well, because when she got back to where we stood waiting, she said, "Hey, Lizzie, why don't you bring Robert in and show him your new gas station?"

CHAPTER TWELVE

We trooped up the porch steps, and Charlie followed Mom into the house. I stopped to pet Edmund Hillary, who was sprawled limply in a patch of sunshine on the porch. Robert had walked over to the edge of the porch, where he stopped, looking through the tangle of honeysuckle vines on the trellis to see if his dad was still in the driveway. When he turned back to me, I was surprised at the troubled look on his face. His eyes were wet, and he blinked hard a few times.

I was bewildered. "What's the matter, Robert? Don't you wanna eat with us?"

Robert sighed but didn't respond for a moment. Instead he slumped down on the porch next to Edmund Hillary and began stroking the cat's sun-warmed fur. The half-grown animal stretched out his four legs, purring a deep, regular purr. "Lizzie, do you promise you won't tell anybody if I tell you a secret? I mean, not anybody, not even your mom and dad?"

I was surprised at Robert's request, but I assumed his secret was some minor confession. I thought he was probably going to admit to having stolen bubble gum from the Safeway store...something like that. That was the only secret anyone had ever told me that had elicited such a promise from me in the past.

"Sure, Robert, I won't tell," I answered.

Robert looked away from me, but not before I was amazed to see two big tears spill from his eyes and run down his cheeks. "Something bad happened to my dad. Something really bad. You can't tell anyone. You promise?"

"Sure, Robert. What happened?"

Robert looked away from me and said, "Well, you know my dad's job. He's a salesman. He drives all over and stuff." He stopped talking and looked back over his shoulder at the tangle of honeysuckle.

"Yeah," I put in by way of encouragement.

"Well, yesterday he was driving real bad and he got in an accident. I guess...he was probably drinking too much. Anyway, he went through a stop sign and hit this farm guy who was driving his truck out in the country. The farmer got out of his truck to look at the dent where my dad ran into him. Dad thought the farmer was coming to get him, so Dad got out of his car to fight him. The farm guy yelled at him and got back in his truck and went home and called the police. Now my dad's company knows, and they fired my dad from his job. That's how come he came home early."

I could hardly take in what Robert was saying. It sounded like a movie. It just didn't seem like something that could happen to anyone I knew. I stared at Robert's miserable face and blurted out, "Are you sure? How do you know?"

"Remember when I went home for lunch?" Robert asked.

"You mean today?"

"Yeah. I went up on the back porch, and I could hear my dad yelling at Mom, and she was yelling and crying. I was scared to go in, but my mom saw me through the door, and she took me in the living room and told me. My dad's just all mad at everybody. He says it's not his fault. He said bad things about the company, and he says he's gonna go beat up that farmer."

That was about the longest speech I'd ever heard Robert make. It seemed to pretty much exhaust him, but he seemed a little relieved, too. He was sitting on the porch now with his back against the railings, and he was petting Edmund Hillary over and over. Untouched by Robert's misery, the cat drowsed and purred and kneaded his claws against Robert's leg.

Though his tears had dried, Robert still looked unhappy and defeated, which made me feel sad and uneasy. I sat there wondering what would happen next in this kind of situation. I had never heard of a father who didn't have a job.

After a little bit, Robert breathed a shaky sigh and said, "Now my dad's over there with only my mom."

I wasn't sure what Robert meant, but the conversation I'd overheard between my mom and dad came back to me. I looked over toward my friend's house. Suddenly it seemed like a scary place. My own house, by contrast, seemed familiar and secure. The warm floorboards of the porch anchored me. The porch railings were the edge of my world.

"You wanna do anything?" I finally asked, not certain if I meant right then or in the coming days.

Robert, though, had long experience with things not going smoothly at home. He sat for a minute longer, cast a long look in the direction of his house, then sighed and said, "Let's go see your new gas station."

CHAPTER THIRTEEN

It felt strange to do something so light-hearted and ordinary in the face of Robert's sobering confession. But then, it always seemed odd when profound or tragic events inserted themselves right into the middle of ordinary daily life. I remembered when my cousin Jim's grandmother lay dying in an upstairs bedroom of her house, and the women in the family stood around in her kitchen and chatted about everyday things while they made lemonade and potato salad. I had been there with my mother, who must have guessed from my bewildered expression how I was feeling, because she patted my head and said quietly, "People have to eat, Honey, and it's better than just sitting and waiting."

I guessed Robert must have had more practice with life's unreasonable dualities, because he got up off the sun-warmed porch and led the way into the house. My new gas station was displayed on our card table in the living room. Its metallic newness drew me, though I felt a little ashamed to leave Robert's trouble so easily behind.

Robert and I circled the table for a while, peeking in the little windows and picking up the miniature people and cars and trucks. Charlie wandered in holding a giant dill pickle in his hand, taking big slurpy bites out of it. Pickle juice was running down his chin, and each time he raised his hand for a bite, the juice ran down his hand and into the cuff of his well-worn shirt. I was glad to see him. He looked comical, and Robert and I both seemed to feel the atmosphere lighten.

"Can I play?" Charlie asked.

"Not while you're eating," I told him. "Go in the kitchen and put down the pickle, wash your face, wash your hands, and dry everything. Then we'll see." Charlie and I had owned a lot of metal toys, and I knew how easily they rusted when they got wet. The toys in our outdoor sandbox were proof of that.

Charlie was not offended. He just stuffed the remainder of the pickle in his mouth and meandered into the kitchen, where we heard him turn on the faucet. He returned a minute later, wiping his hands on his pants, his mouth so crammed with pickle that he was having trouble chewing. Pickle juice spurted from his mouth as he tried to bite down.

"Okay, let's see your hands. Are they dry?"

"Yeb," Charlie answered around the pickle.

"Okay, you can play. Just don't spit on everything."

Charlie and Robert and I spent a peaceful half-hour then, playing with my new gas station, running the little people up and down on the elevator, filling up the trucks with the tiny gasoline hose, and running the cars around on the ramps. Robert seemed so much his normal self. The bad things that had happened to his father were, for me, distant and unreal. How could Robert just stand there, fiddling with a little red truck, examining it with apparent interest? He wasn't crying. He didn't look worried. I tried to imagine how I would feel if my own father were in that situation, but it was too much of a stretch. My dad was an architect and a building contractor and my mom said he was his own boss, so he couldn't get fired anyway, could he? If anything, he was the one who did the firing.

As a matter of fact, I remembered clearly one evening when I was five. My dad had come home and said to my mom, "I had to fire a man today." He had seemed troubled about it, and at the time I had assumed that he had actually had to set a man on fire. It had seemed harsh to me, no matter what the fellow had done, but I had had such complete faith in my father that, well, if he had found it necessary to burn someone up, he must have had a good reason.

But now Robert's father had been fired, and there was my friend, playing with cars and looking just as he always looked…focused and absorbed. He must have been a little on edge, though, because while he was standing with his back to the kitchen door, my mom came out from the kitchen and said, "Anybody getting hungry?"

Robert was startled, and he jumped back, and, just for a moment, looked really frightened. Then he laughed a soft, nervous laugh, looking relieved and a little embarrassed. Charlie stared at him curiously and said, "Geez, Robert, take it easy."

Feeling uncomfortable for Robert, I tried to help him slide past the awkward moment by asking, "Mom, can we eat at the Rambler?"

The Rambler was the sprawling cobblestone ballroom and restaurant on the eastern shore of St. Luke Lake. By St. Luke's standards, it qualified as a fancy restaurant, and the adjoining ballroom was a true landmark, having hosted many of the great dance bands of the thirties and forties. Whenever we went to the restaurant, I peeked through the big double doors into the dimly lit ballroom, lured by the sheen of the expansive, polished hardwood dance floor. The empty ballroom always conveyed an aura of hushed expectancy, as though waiting for the ghost dancers to return in their long dresses and glittering jewelry, their tuxedoes and dazzling shirts. My parents had their own memories of those days and had told Charlie and me stories of splendid evenings and marvelous dance bands and the tight camaraderie of a generation that had survived a depression and then gone through a war. On my mother's dresser there was a black and white picture of the two of them, elegantly dressed, looking very excited and very young. They were standing just outside the big double doors of the ballroom.

In the fifties, the Moose Lodge still hosted dances there in the summertime, and once or twice a summer our family would attend. I was always captivated by the unfamiliar smell of beer and the equally unfamiliar experience of adults being loud and rather boisterous. My own parents just stuck with Charlie and me, dancing only with each other and with us. When my dad and I danced, I stood on the tops of his feet while he took little swaying steps around the dance floor. My family seemed like a little island of decency and reason in an otherwise slightly decadent and doubtful place.

The Rambler restaurant sang its own siren song. Children who went there with their families always found their attention riveted to the mural painted along the upper portion of the restaurant walls. It was an ocean scene populated liberally with beautiful mermaids, all of whom were naked from the waist up. The mural alone was enough to give the restaurant a slightly forbidden air, but the building itself seemed to breathe its own exotic atmosphere. The cobblestone walls seemed to exude a damp, chilly, lime-laden sweat that, for me, at least, helped define the whole experience of the Rambler. I loved going there. It was a foreign place, a grown-up place. It was like sneaking into the circus.

My mother and father liked the Rambler, too, so when I asked Mom if we could eat there for my birthday, she struck a pose and answered, "Well, this birthday just goes on and on! I'd better go and prepare myself for the birthday feast!" She hugged me and ruffled Robert's hair and went off to her room to change clothes.

I had a moment of total satisfaction, thinking, "Boy, my birthday is going great!" Then I caught sight of Robert, staring after my mother blankly. He looked at me and gave me a tired little smile. Every time I thought of his anguished confession on the porch, it caught me up short, but each time I remembered it, it seemed a little less real

Part of the unreality stemmed from knowing something—something serious—that my parents didn't know. Robert's situation didn't seem like a suitable preoccupation for a child. Even I, a child, knew that much. I felt like I should somehow tie Robert's problem up in a handkerchief and hand the whole package over to my mom. "Here. Take this. Somebody handed it to me by mistake." Most of the time, though, I just forgot about it.

CHAPTER FOURTEEN

About five thirty or so, Charlie and I heard Dad's car pulling up the drive. We ran to the back door to meet him, the way we did every afternoon. "Daddy, guess what! We're all going to eat out at the Rambler! Robert, too!"

"Great! Who's paying?" Dad was grinning as he leaned over to hug Charlie and me. Robert stood shyly off to the side, watching the three of us together. Mom appeared from the bedroom. She was wearing a white summer dress with big red flowers splashed around on it, and she'd applied lipstick and rouge. I could smell the almond scent of Jergen's hand lotion. My dad looked at her and whistled.

Robert was looking at Mom, too, and said, unexpectedly, "Gee, you look real pretty, Mrs. Harris."

We all turned to stare at Robert, taken aback by his sudden declaration. Although he talked easily with Charlie and me, he was usually pretty shy and tongue-tied around adults—even around other kids. My mother recovered herself and said, "Why, thank you, Robert!"

By then Robert seemed to realize what he had spontaneously blurted out, and I could tell he was a little panicky, blushing furiously and backing nervously away from my mom in case she decided to hug him.

Mom recognized his discomfort, and she began to bustle around the kitchen, straightening up the counter and saying, "Okay, where's my purse?"

It really did feel like a party now, with my mom dressed up and my dad breezy and dashing. Even Charlie seemed excited, hopping from one foot to the other, announcing, "I can't wait! I'm ordering a hamburger!" This came as no surprise to any of us, as Charlie had never ordered anything but a hamburger in his life.

In his own subdued way, Robert, too, was caught up in the spirit of celebration. He was grinning a little uncertainly, and he kept glancing from one person to another, looking for clues as to how to behave.

My dad held up the car keys, jingling them together, and said, "Let's get this show on the road!" We herded ourselves out the door, Dad holding the screen open for Mom but letting it bang shut on Charlie. They had perfected a little comic routine in which Dad would wait until Charlie was behind him, and Charlie would plant one foot in the doorway, so the screen door would bang against his toe. Then he'd launch into his act, yelping and holding his nose and squinting hard to produce a hint of tears. He was pretty convincing, unless you'd witnessed the whole scenario dozens of times. As it was, Mom just laughed, and Robert and I rolled our eyes at each other.

As we were piling into the station wagon, it occurred to me that my parents weren't carrying a present. I hesitated. Not wanting to appear greedy, but at the same time unwilling to risk an oversight, I ventured, "Mom, when do I get my last present?"

My dad widened his eyes in mock amazement and said, "You get *another* present?"

"Daddy, it's in the plan! Mom and I have it all planned. There's one more present. Right, Mom? There's one more present?"

Mom laughed at my brazenness. "Well, yes, Honey. I think that was the plan. One more present. When we get home."

I had no problem with waiting until we got home. Actually, I had been feeling a little self-conscious about opening up my last gift in the middle of a busy restaurant. I had imagined how it would look: me opening up a gift-wrapped box and pulling out a gleaming hunting knife. I'd imagined it might cause some curious whispers, perhaps even some disapproving stares. Opening it at home would be better.

It was about a ten-minute drive around the east end of the lake to the Rambler. As we circled the lake, I asked, "What do you like to order at the Rambler, Robert?"

There was a little pause. Then Robert answered, "I don't know. I've never been there before."

I was incredulous. "You've never eaten at the Rambler? Really? Not even once?"

My mother jumped hurriedly into the conversation. "Oh, Lizzie, lots of families don't eat there. Some of our friends don't care for it. They don't like the food. And some people say they always have to wait for a table.'

"Well, we've never had to wait!" maintained Charlie.

I knew as well as Charlie that the Rambler wasn't all that crowded, but I could hear the gentle undertone of warning in my mother's voice, and I understood, albeit belatedly, that the idea was to spare Robert's feelings. I fished around for something to say.

"Oh, yeah, it is crowded sometimes. And sometimes it's cold in there."

Robert had recovered, and he said gamely, "I guess I'll just have whatever you're having, Lizzie." Robert was trying hard to be a good birthday guest, and he was so transparently vulnerable that I felt like hugging him. That unfamiliar impulse made me so uncomfortable that I searched around frantically for a way to refocus the conversation.

"Well, Charlie likes the hamburgers a lot," I finally offered.

"Yeah," Charlie chimed in. "I'm havin' a hamburger."

"Surprise, surprise," Dad commented.

When we pulled into the parking lot, Robert stared solemnly out of the car windows at the big brass-doored entrance to the Rambler. A man in a suit and a woman in a summery dress were going in. Robert looked down at his shorts and striped T-shirt. He asked, "Do you have to be dressed up?"

"Robert!" I was grinning. "Look at me! Look at Charlie! You look better'n us!"

My mother looked at us as though noticing for the first time that Charlie and I were wearing pretty unusual clothing. I was still in my jeans and Hopalong Cassidy suspenders, and Charlie was in shorts and his completely worn-out long-sleeved shirt. Mom sighed, then gave a little laugh and said, "Come on, Robert. I'm going to pretend that you're my real child, and we're just taking these two along as a favor."

That seemed to make Robert relax. It must have been obvious to him that he was the best dressed of the three of us. Still, I noticed he stuck pretty close to Mom. The five of us trooped happily through those big brass doors and on through the lobby, where I noticed that it actually was kind of cold. We entered the restaurant and stood by the cash register waiting for the hostess to seat us.

Robert was gazing around the brightly lit restaurant, taking in the white linen tablecloths, the sparkling glassware, the gleaming chandelier, and the white-coated waiters. And then I saw his eyes get even wider and his mouth drop open, and I knew he'd spotted the half-naked mermaids. He stared at them for a minute, and then he poked me in the ribs and hissed, "Lizzie, do you see what I see?"

"I know," I whispered back. I felt guilty and embarrassed, as though I were somehow responsible.

"They're bare-naked!"

"Yeah, I know."

"And your *parents* come here!"

"Well…they like the steaks," I finished lamely.

The hostess came then and took us to a big, round table and pulled out chairs for us, handing us each an enormous, gold-tasseled menu. Robert took his politely, although I was pretty sure he didn't know what it was at first. The only menu he'd probably ever seen was printed above the counter at Bert's Burgers next to the Orpheum Theater.

When Robert opened his menu and realized what it was, he looked up and down the columns, furrowing his forehead and biting his lip. I wondered if he was worrying about the prices.

My dad glanced over at my friend, then announced cheerfully, "Well, the rule is, at birthday dinners we all order exactly what we want! What'll you have, Lizzie?"

"I think I'll have a fried egg sandwich. And grape pop."

Charlie added, "A burger for me."

"Shocking," said Mom, smiling tolerantly.

"I'd like a hamburger, too, if that's okay," said Robert.

"Absolutely okay," my father said. It crossed my mind for a moment how kind my parents were being to Robert, and how easily and casually they always seemed to know just what to say or do to set him at ease. I looked from my mom to my dad and felt an uncharacteristic rush of gratitude. And Charlie. Good old Charlie. He held no prejudice against anyone or anything, and the only trait he found objectionable was meanness. I wondered, just for a moment, if Charlie were a better person than I. That thought was mildly astonishing to me—astonishing that it would have occurred to me at all, and astonishing that it was probably true.

My parents ordered steak, which must have reminded Robert of our earlier conversation about the mermaids. Emerging from behind his giant menu, he started looking around the restaurant, pretending an earnest curiosity about his surroundings. My parents were chatting and laughing together, affecting an unawareness of Robert's gaze. Charlie, however, followed Robert's mesmerized stare to the murals overhead. He looked at one rather spectacular mermaid for a moment and then, as casually as if he were commenting on the weather, proclaimed, "Those are the biggest bosoms I ever saw!"

I stared at Charlie in mortified shock. Robert's face was turning crimson. My parents, after an initial moment of surprise, broke into such laughter that tears were threatening to spill from my mother's eyes. When my dad caught his breath, he asked, "So, Charlie, how many bosoms have you seen?"

"Well, Mom...," Charlie began, but Mom cut him off.

"I think we've pretty much covered the subject of bosoms for tonight. Let's move on to something else."

And so we did. It was a wonderful dinner, really. The dining room sparkled around us. We all laughed a lot, and everything seemed elegant and welcoming and bright. Robert and Charlie and I recounted the Peter Pan movie to Dad, and the retelling seemed to bring back some of the magic of the afternoon. Dad chewed his steak and nodded and smiled his way through our story. Charlie and Robert thought their hamburgers were delicious, and Dad said that that was high praise for a hamburger, since Charlie had sampled hamburgers from St. Luke in Iowa to our grandma's house in California.

We had such a good time together that for a while I forgot that my best present was still to come. As we were leaving the Rambler, though, my thoughts returned to my schedule of presents, and I rode home wriggling in anticipation.

CHAPTER FIFTEEN

While we were climbing out of the station wagon, my mom put her hand on Robert's shoulder and said, "Robert, I think you have time to join us for cake before Lizzie opens her last present. Come on in." There was a cheerful firmness in her voice, and she kept her hand on Robert's shoulder, steering him up the porch steps toward the kitchen. I knew she was saving Robert from the problem of deciding whether or not he could stay. He did look back over his shoulder as we went through the screen door, but he couldn't resist the tide of familial goodwill that swept him along.

Once inside, Mom sailed around the kitchen, gathering up plates, silverware, napkins, and glasses and arranging everything on the table. Then she ordered us all to sit down, and she ceremoniously carried my chocolate layer cake from the counter, placing it in front of me with a little flourish. My dad put the eight candles in the top, spacing them far apart so they'd be harder to blow out.

"Ready?" Dad said, and I grinned and nodded. He lit the candles, and everybody sang "Happy Birthday." I sang, too, just because I felt foolish sitting there doing nothing while so much attention was focused on me.

Then Charlie said, "Okay, make your wish!" That brought me up short. I had forgotten about the wish. I hesitated to waste a wish on my knife, because I was pretty certain I'd get that anyway. And I had focused so intently in recent days on my desire for that knife that all other potential wishes had fallen by the wayside.

"Hurry up!" said Charlie. "The candles are dripping down on the frosting!"

Feeling under pressure, I closed my eyes and made a silent wish. "I wish Robert's dad would get a job where he makes enough money and doesn't have to travel around to other towns." I had no idea where that uncharacteristically unselfish wish had come from. It had just appeared, full-blown and unbidden, in my thoughts. I hadn't even been thinking about Robert's dad since we'd left for the Rambler. I opened my eyes, blew out my candles, and was immediately overcome by a vague uneasiness. Had I muffed an important step in my birthday celebration? The wish business had all flashed by too quickly, and I hoped I wouldn't somehow be penalized for my unintended generosity. Too late now.

My mother was cutting the cake. "Okay, Robbity, now I need to explain about birthday cakes in our family," Mom said, sounding ominously like a person about to make a serious, possibly lengthy, speech. Putting a big slab of cake down in front of Robert, she went on, "In our family, we celebrate birthdays with money cakes, with coins between the layers. When you find a coin, you can keep it, or you can give it to the birthday person."

"Fat chance!" commented Charlie. "I'd like a really big piece, Mom!"

Mom awarded Charlie a look of mock disapproval and continued, "You have to actually eat the cake. You can't just keep disassembling pieces for the money. Be careful when you bite down not to bite on the money. We don't want to end up at the dentist's on Lizzie's birthday."

We all started poking our forks between the layers of our cake. Everybody found at least one coin. I was relieved when Robert found a dime and a quarter. I knew if he'd found nothing, he would have pretended not to care, and for some reason that would have made me really sad. As it was, he reacted with a solemn respect, carefully setting the coins on the edge of his plate until he finished his cake. When his plate was clean, he picked up the frosting-smeared coins and handed them to me. "Happy birthday, Lizzie," he said, and he smiled.

CHAPTER SIXTEEN

And right then was when my birthday stopped being perfect. First there was the sound of loud heavy footsteps crossing the back porch, followed by a loud, insistent banging on the door. Robert's eyes flew open, and for a moment he looked frozen. Then he was all quick motion, sliding out of his chair, saying, "That's my dad. I better go."

Both my parents rose quickly from their own chairs. My mother's color was rising, and she put a protective hand on Robert's shoulder as she walked him to the back door. My father was fixing a smile on his face as he strode behind them.

"Hey, Paul," my Dad said heartily, trying to engineer the situation into a friendly neighborhood encounter. "Come on in for some birthday cake."

Robert's dad was trying to respond in kind, but was having a rough go of it. An angry impatience pressed up behind his eyes, and he seemed to struggle to focus his thoughts. "Ah, no, thanks, but it's time...Robert's been gone for hours now, and he's got some jobs over at home. It's gettin' late."

I could tell my mother was reluctant to let Robert go. She had her hands on both his shoulders now, and she stood close behind him. She tried once more with Mr. Sherwood. "Well, we've sure been enjoying your son today! He's such a gentleman! I'm afraid he puts Lizzie and Charlie to shame! Sure you can't join us for some cake?"

But Robert's dad was already backing unsteadily across our porch, waving a hand in dismissal. As he turned to go down the steps, he called back. "C'mon, Robert. You've been gone all day, for Chrissake."

Robert shrugged away from my mother. "It's okay, Mrs. Harris. I gotta go. Thanks for takin' me out to dinner. I had a great time. G'nite. Happy birthday, Lizzie." He pushed open the screen door and went out, the door banging shut behind him. About halfway across the porch he stopped and turned around. Looking back at us, he smiled an odd little smile and said, "That was one of the best days I ever had."

By then all four of us were standing at the back door, and we all watched in silence as Robert's small, resigned little figure trudged away across the back yard. When he was almost home, Mom called out, "G'nite, Sweetie," but Robert didn't seem to hear. He stepped into the rectangle of shadow that was his back door and disappeared.

CHAPTER SEVENTEEN

My own family just stood there for a minute, staring silently at the door that had swallowed Robert up. Perhaps we were waiting for some sound from Robert's house, but there were only the soothing noises of a summer evening. A few birds were chirping in the backyard elms, and I could hear the gritty rattle of metal roller skate wheels crossing the sidewalk cracks somewhere down the block. The peaceful smells of honeysuckle and climbing roses and Mr. Hibbs' freshly cut grass drifted on a small breeze.

The tranquility of it all seeped into the four of us as we stood there, and after a minute or so, we all kind of gave ourselves a mental shake, looked at each other, and broke again into easy chatter. My dad put a friendly hand on my head and said, "I think we have some birthday left to go."

He steered Charlie and me back to our places at the table. We both had cake to finish up, and although I felt twinges of conscience over my lack of concern for Robert, I was already enjoying a rising tide of excitement over my final present. When the cake was finished and the plates were cleared away, I could stand the suspense no longer. From a practical standpoint, I wanted to get my knife while there was ample time to admire it before bedtime. I put my hands down flat on the table and demanded, "Okay! Can I please have my last present now?"

My parents looked at each other, raising their eyebrows in mock disapproval. I could detect, though, the element of smug satisfaction, their certainty that they had found the perfect gift, and that their child would be delighted.

"Well, let's see...," began my father. "I'm just not quite sure how to do this." He paused, considering. "I think...Lizzie, why don't you and Charlie go sit on the front porch steps. Mom and I will bring your present out there."

I felt a little flutter of uncertainty in my stomach. Why the front porch? Why not right here at the kitchen table? Was a knife somehow an outdoor present, like a bow-and-arrow set?

The gnawing uneasiness continued as Charlie and I went through the house and out onto the front porch. We looked around and, seeing no one, we sat down on the top step. We'd been waiting about two minutes when we heard the big cellar storm doors being opened from below. Then there were some muffled laughs, some banging and thumping sounds, and finally, the unmistakable "brrrrring" of a bicycle bell.

Astonished, I flew down the steps and around the corner of the house. There, coming toward me, were my mother and father, grinning crazily and pushing between them a brand new blue and white bicycle. In addition to the bell, a chrome bike light gleamed above the handlebars. Multicolored plastic streamers fluttered from the handle grips. My parents wheeled the bicycle around to the front sidewalk, and my dad pushed the kickstand down with his foot. And there, parked in front of me, book-ended by my happily expectant parents, was my final present. My new bicycle.

I was stunned. I'd been so certain that I'd be getting that knife that I had rehearsed a response to no other present. A bicycle was obviously a wonderful gift, an expensive gift, a gift that, even as taken aback as I was, I could appreciate. But what about my knife? What about all the plans I'd made that required that very knife? But a bicycle! A bicycle was such a big present that it never would have occurred to me to ask for one. I did know how to ride a bike (I had learned on my cousin Mary's old clunker) but I would never have imagined having one of my own, one that I could ride whenever I wanted.

Emerging gradually from my cloud of confusion, I noticed Charlie's dazzled expression and my parents' expectant faces. They were obviously waiting for what they assumed would be my rapturous reaction, even as I was trying to sort out what my reaction actually was. My parents must have interpreted my wide-eyed silence as speechless joy. Finally I managed to blurt out, "Wow! It's...should I...can I ride it?"

My father was as close to giddy as I had ever seen him. He was fussing with the seat, loosening it with a little wrench so he could adjust the height. "What do ya' think, Lizzie? Let's boost you up here so we can try it on for size."

There was a lot of enthusiasm being displayed. Charlie was bouncing around, yelping with excitement. Dad was hoisting me on and off the seat, keeping up a running commentary. "Okay, just one notch lower. Okay, up one more time. How's that feel? Do your feet touch the pedals? See, this leg should be almost straight down when the pedal's down. And then, to stop, you just pedal backwards. Did you practice that on Mary's bike? Okay, there you go, kiddo!"

So, with all that activity, my mixed feelings went unnoticed, and I at least had the presence of mind to feel relieved about that. I realized the magnitude of the gift my parents had given me. It was just that I had been so sure about the knife. It was as though I'd actually had it in my possession and had somehow lost it. I was floundering, and now I was trying to react as I felt my family expected me to in response to this new and totally unanticipated largesse.

"Well, where should I go?" I asked. How did a person get started being a bike rider? A bike owner?

My question, along with my obvious uncertainty, triggered some businesslike, organizational nerve in my mother. She got up from the bottom step where she'd been perched, enjoying the show, and came toward us, holding her hands in front of her, palms front, fingers spread, in a gesture that clearly said, "Okay, let's just outline a few ground rules."

She began, "Daddy and I think we should have a few rules about your new bike, Honey. It's just to keep you safe. Like no riding in the dark. And no riding across any streets without telling us where you're going. And no riding in the street until you've had a little more practice."

By now, my attention was being drawn effectively away from any lingering thoughts about the present I'd been counting on. After all, there was the shiny bicycle itself, right in front of me. There was my mom, happily rambling on about bike rules. There was my dad, bending down to administer some final tightening and adjusting. And there was Charlie, playing with the light and the bell and the streamers, and so obviously happy and excited for me that I felt a wave of affection mixed with guilt.

My dad was rubbing his hands together, anticipating the fruits of his labor. His usual methodical calm had given way to a barely controlled glee. "Why don't you take it for a little spin, Lizzie?"

I felt oddly nervous performing for my family, but I could hardly have thrown a wet blanket on all that generous goodwill, so I took the handlebars in my hand, kicked the kickstand up, and walked my new bike down to the front sidewalk. Stepping awkwardly up on the pedals, I wobbled down the walk for a few yards before I leveled off. After that, though, I managed to glide along pretty smoothly. I knew some of the tricks that you needed to know to ride on the sidewalk. Tree roots were the biggest threat. The old oaks and elms and maples planted shortsightedly close to the walks sent out roots that gradually rose up under the cement and turned flat sidewalks into a series of crooked ramps and drop-offs that could send you sprawling My cousin Mary had advised me, "Just hit all the bumps straight on, not at an angle. Same for railroad tracks. *Especially* railroad tracks." So that evening as I rode down the sidewalk, I watched for obstacles and did my best to approach them head on.

When I came to the corner, I wasn't sure what to do, so I got off my bike, turned it around, got back on, and rode back to my own driveway, where my family welcomed me back with cheers and applause. I was pleased and embarrassed at the same time, so I just stood there, flushed and grinning and unable to think of anything to say.

My parents seemed to feel that the festivities were wrapping up. A curtain fell on my birthday as my dad said, "Well, you look pretty snazzy on that bike, Honey. Why don't you ride it a few more times, and then put it in the garage for the night." Then he gathered up his tools and, joined by my mother, headed back towards the cellar door. They were smiling and chatting easily together, no doubt congratulating themselves on the wonderful birthday they'd provided for me.

CHAPTER EIGHTEEN

It really had been a nearly perfect day, but now that all the excitement was dying down, I had a minute to sort out my emotions. I was trying to balance the genuine pleasure I felt over my new bicycle with the nagging disappointment over not getting my knife. I realized the potential of my bicycle for opening up new avenues of adventure. I considered it only a matter of a few weeks before I'd be able to persuade my parents that I could ride safely on the streets and travel farther than a block from home.

But since I hadn't received the knife for my birthday, I knew the chances were pretty nonexistent that I'd ever get it at all, at least not from my parents. After all, I'd made my wishes pretty clear.

I stood quietly by my bicycle, running my hand absentmindedly over the seat. Charlie stood beside me, looking from me to the bicycle and back again. He must have realized that I didn't seem nearly as jubilant as he would have expected, because he suddenly put his hands on his hips and asked impatiently, "What's the matter? Don't you like it?"

Feeling a little guilty, I looked up and answered, "Well, yeah, I do like it. It's great. It's just…you know, Charlie…I did really want that hunting knife. You know, that one with the sheath and…."

"What?" Charlie was incredulous. "What?" Are you kidding? Are you *crazy?*" Charlie was actually pacing, waving his arms. He stopped and threw his hands in the air. "Yes…you…are…*crazy!*" He stalked off, muttering and shaking his head like an old man. When he reached the front steps, he turned back around and, circling a finger around his ear, he repeated, "*Crazy!*" Then he stomped up the stairs and disappeared into the house, leaving me and my bicycle standing on the front lawn in the slanting light of a beautiful July evening.

I felt muddled and tired and restless all at once. The day had churned along with such a happy succession of events, and now there was only quiet and a sense of mild abandonment. Walking my bike up close to the flowerbed beneath the porch railing, I carefully parked it, making sure the kickstand supported it before letting go of the handlebars. Then I stood there a minute, looking vacantly about.

It must have been about eight o'clock, still light out, and I decided I'd take a little walk, just to be by myself for a while. I headed down the sidewalk toward the lake. As I passed Robert's house I looked up at his front porch, but there was no sign of Robert or of anyone else. I continued on, past the Hibbs' house, past Mrs. Krebb's house, across the street and on down two houses to Grace Logan's big old Victorian home.

Grace and her house were suited to each other. Grace, like the house she lived in, was comfortable, sturdy, well kept, and lightly touched with whimsy. That July evening I spotted her perched on her top step with a big metal bowl of green beans beside her. She was snapping the ends off the beans and dropping them into a big saucepan on the next step down.

"Hi, Lizzie! What's up?" she called down to me. Grace being Grace, I knew her question was sincere. Grace had a genuine interest in my life and in the lives of Charlie and Robert. She really did want to know what was up. She knew what books we were reading, what movies we had seen, what we thought about our teachers, and how we felt about things in general. Best of all, she never tried to tell us that we actually felt some other way. If I told her I hated school, she accepted it as a fact. She never said, "Oh, no, you don't really hate school. You love school."

She smiled a welcoming smile and patted the place beside her on the top step. "C'mon up here. I want to hear about your birthday."

I wasn't sure I felt like talking, but I couldn't think of a polite way to decline, so I trudged up the steps and sat down next to her.

"How was that movie? Did you like it? Did Robert think it was like the book?" Grace always asked specific questions that you couldn't shrug off. Robert's dad had once told us that Grace only liked talking to children because she was old and lonely and bored. I didn't think that was true. Grownups like that never remembered what kids said from one day to the next. Grace remembered everything about us.

My mother told me that Grace was somewhere around sixty, and I wasn't sure if that was old or not. And I knew that she was lonely once in a while, because a few months earlier, I'd asked her. She had considered the question for a moment and answered, "Lonely? Hmmmm." Then there was another long pause while she looked off into space, her head cocked to one side. Then she said, "Well, I guess I get a little lonely about once a week, usually on Sunday afternoons. In a little town like this, you know, Honey, Sunday afternoons are pretty much family time. And since my husband died, and my son and daughter grew up and moved to Des Moines, the house does seem kind of big and empty and quiet on Sundays. But, by golly, I'm working on some schemes to de-lonelify myself!"

She'd stopped there and looked down at me to see if I was still listening, so, of course, I'd said, "What schemes?"

Apparently I'd asked a question that she'd been hoping to have the chance to answer. Her face brightened into a grin, and she responded happily. "Okay, then, scheme one: I'm making scrapbooks for my son and daughter of all their growing-up years. That's fun for me. I sit there with all those pictures around me, and I feel like I'm back in the pictures with my kids young again. And scheme two: Oh, this is great!" Grace paused for dramatic effect, then leaned closer and said in a half-whisper, "I'm getting a *television*!"

"Really? When?" My mouth had dropped open, and I must have looked nakedly envious, because Grace had laughed and hugged me and said, "Next week! And I want you and your family and your pal Robert to come over and watch it with me."

That conversation had taken place the previous March, and Grace had indeed bought a television, and Robert and Charlie and I had spent more than a few Saturday mornings on our stomachs on Grace's living room floor, munching Grace's oatmeal cookies and watching Roy Rogers and Sky King and Buster Brown and the Lone Ranger.

And now, on that warm July evening, when Grace asked me about the movie, and about the rest of my birthday, I sat there and, calmed by the fragrant breeze and the musical "plink, plink" of string beans hitting the metal pan, I told her everything. I told her about the movie, and how much we'd liked it, and how Robert had said it was much better than the book. Grace said, "You know, I loved that book. Actually, I just read it last year, when I found out that they were making a movie out of it. Now I guess I'll have to borrow a child somewhere and go see that movie."

"You can borrow me," I offered. "Do you care that I've already seen it?"

"Of course not," Grace reassured me. "You can tell me when the good parts are coming. So…it's a deal."

I was quiet then, and Grace, noticing my less-than-jubilant mood, said, "Well, how was the rest of your birthday? Did you get everything on your list?" She paused. "Any disappointments?"

"Well, I did get a real good present. I got my own bicycle. A brand new one. It's blue. It has a light and a bell and streamers coming out of the handlebars."

"Wow! A bike! That's wonderful! You can ride all over town!"

"Yup, I guess so," I responded, wondering idly how long it would be before my parents let me ride quite that far.

"So," said Grace, "what's the trouble then?"

"Well, I kind of wanted a hunting knife. I had one all picked out."

"A hunting knife?" Grace repeated.

"Yeah, with a sheath." I looked up at Grace. "And this little belt thing so you could strap it on your leg down by your ankle."

"Well, uh huh. That would have been a good present too."

Grace and I sat together in a comfortable silence, looking out at the street. I knew Grace understood, and I was grateful.

After a while she said, "You know, it's funny. When I was nine, I wanted a bow and arrow set. But that was in the year…let's see…1899, and little girls in those days, at least, little girls in Dubuque, Iowa, well, we wore flouncy dresses and big bows in our hair, and we got paint kits and dolls and embroidery sets for our birthdays. My mother was embarrassed that I even wanted a bow and arrow set. So one day, when I was twenty-two years old, I went out and bought myself an archery set, and, by golly, I got pretty good at it!"

I digested this information for a minute, and then I asked, "Do you still have it?"

Grace got a faraway look on her face. "No, Honey, I don't. When my son Martin was seven or eight—about your age, come to think of it—he found my bow and some of the arrows in the attic, and he tried them out, and he accidentally shot himself in the thumb somehow. I know that sounds impossible. I can't, to this day, figure out quite how he did it. But I worried that if he could manage to shoot himself in the thumb, he could shoot his baby sister in the eye without too much trouble, so I got rid of the archery set. But by then

I had Martin and Alice to play with, and they were lots more fun anyway."

I sat for a minute, wondering if I'd still want a hunting knife when I was twenty-two, but the idea of my ever being twenty-two was too much even for my imagination. I guess Grace must have seen that I was still a little blue, because she gave my knee a pat and said, "Hey, how about we go see that movie on Sunday afternoon? Oh, wait, no, my cooking club is making coq au vin on Sunday. That's French for drunken chicken."

"Really?" This was interesting. "How do you get the chicken drunk?"

"Well, I don't know yet. I guess that's the fun part."

Grace was grinning, so I knew she was pulling my leg. "Don't worry. We'll find another time to see that movie."

That seemed like a good time to be on my way, so I stood up and said, "Well, I guess I'll go down to our dock for a while." I hopped down the steps. "Seeya, Grace!"

"G'nite, Honey! Come see me soon!"

I could hear the understanding and the sympathy in Grace's voice. I felt comforted and cheered, and I turned around two or three times to wave back at her.

CHAPTER NINETEEN

It was only about another block to the lake from Grace's house. It was soothing, walking under the canopy of those old trees, with the sidewalk giving up its heat from the day. When I got to the lake I walked along the grassy strip overlooking the little bluff until I came to the steps leading down to our dock. I went down the steps and walked out to the end of the dock. Sitting on the edge of the plank bench, I took off my cowboy boots and socks and put them neatly under the bench. Then I sat down on the side of the dock and dangled my feet in the water.

I guess I sat there for fifteen minutes or so, watching the sailboats gliding silently along and the speedboats tracing foamy channels through the water. After that I got a little bored and spent another few minutes clambering around on the Indian trails.

When I came to our secret cave I decided to stop off to rest a bit. The cave wasn't really very comfortable—it was really just a clay-walled indentation about the size of Grace's new console television—but it was cozy and private. If you moved a few branches in front of the opening, you could sit in there and be nearly invisible to anyone passing down on the shore.

I scrunched down and turned around, backing my way into the opening. Then I sat down, leaned back against the cool clay, and closed my eyes. It had been a long day, full of activity and excitement and emotion, and the fatigue that had been gathering in on me finally found the occasion to settle. Within a minute or two I dozed off, and I didn't wake up until I heard the drowning bell.

What I had forgotten was that I'd left my socks and cowboy boots parked out there under the bench at the end of the dock, and those were the boots and socks my dad had found when he'd come down to the dock looking for me after Grace had told him, "I think Lizzie was feeling a little blue. She went down to your dock to be by herself for a while."

When my father found my empty boots I don't think he panicked immediately, but he was pretty worried, and then when I failed to respond to his increasingly anxious calls, he began to get pretty scared. He told me the next day that he'd walked along the beach about a block and a half in either direction from our dock, calling my name the whole time. He must have walked right past me twice, and I never heard a thing.

When Dad got no answer from me, he felt desperation creeping over him, and, not knowing what else to do, he ran up the steps and headed for the bell. On his way he encountered Grace, who had gotten worried and come down to the lake to investigate. My dad had told her that he had found my boots, but that I wasn't in them. He was going to ring the bell to gather people to look for me, and Grace should go back to get my mom.

And that brings me back to the point where I began. After I appeared, and after all the excitement had begun to subside, my family walked back home together, Charlie and I leading the way, and Mom and Dad following along behind. When we got home, there was my new bicycle, parked neatly by the front porch. Something about its presence there seemed to convey a silent rebuke, as though it were saying, "How could you cause such trouble when your parents just gave you this beautiful bike?"

My dad looked at it, shook his head, and said quietly, "Better put your bicycle in the garage, Lizzie." He sounded tired and disappointed, which made me feel just awful. I walked my new bicycle up the driveway and parked it carefully in the back of the garage. When I came out, my dad was waiting for me. He pulled the garage door down and then, to my astonishment, he leaned over and picked me up and held me.

"Well, I'm sure glad we didn't get an ordinary, boring little girl. What fun would that be, anyway?" And with that he carried me all the way across the yard and the back porch and into the house and right up the stairs to my room, where he finally set me down. I was so taken aback (my father never picked me up anymore, much less carried me all that way) that I could think of nothing to say. When he put me down he said, "Well, you better get yourself ready for bed. And you, too, Charlie."

Charlie, it seemed, had quietly followed us up the stairs, keeping a careful distance behind us. After we were in bed, he told me that he'd been afraid Dad was carrying me upstairs to give me a spanking, even though neither Charlie nor I had been spanked for years.

"I thought he was carrying you so you couldn't escape," was how Charlie put it.

But when Mom and Dad had come to tuck us in, they hadn't really seemed angry with me at all. They were quiet, and they seemed serious and worn out. My father sat down on the edge of my bed and said, "Lizzie, Mom and I were really worried that something had happened to you. You've got to remember—when you run off someplace by yourself, you need to tell us where you're going and when you'll be back. So we've decided, to remind you, you can't ride your new bike for one week. We were going to say that you couldn't play with Robert, either, but we decided there was no point in punishing poor Robert. He's got enough trouble as it is. So, okay?"

I recognized this as a solemn moment, and I tried to match my parents' sober demeanor. "Okay, Daddy. I'm sorry. I didn't mean to fall asleep." And then, belatedly, I took in what my father had said about Robert's having enough trouble. I blurted out, "Daddy, something bad happened to Robert's dad." I hesitated. I was torn between my loyalty to Robert and my feeling, born of long experience, that if I could just tell my parents about my friend's situation, that they could somehow fix it. At the very least, I wouldn't be carrying it around all by myself.

My dad sat there quietly for a minute, his elbows on his knees. I think he was internally debating how comfortably a newly minted eight-year-old could deal with adult misfortune. Finally, he said, "Yeah, we know, Honey. I ran into Chief Galsworthy downtown this afternoon. He told me about the accident and...everything. So, we'll just be extra nice to Robert and his mom now. Their family might be in for some tough times for a while."

"But he has to have a job, right? What if he's home all the time? They have to have money, don't they? Can't he just get a new job?"

"Oh, I'm sure he'll try. You know, Lizzie, he's not all bad, but he has a drinking problem. Do you know what that is?"

"He gets drunk and does stupid stuff, and it makes him be mean, and he trips on stuff and falls down." My knowledge of drunkenness was a mixture of my observations of Mr. Sherwood and scenes from cartoons and movies I'd seen.

My dad suppressed a smile. "Well, that's ...pretty close, I guess."

I considered the problem. "Why doesn't he just not drink beer, then?" Beer was the only alcoholic beverage that I could actually name.

My dad took a minute to respond. "Honey, I don't think anybody knows the answer to that question. Some people just get started drinking, and they can't seem to stop."

"Daddy?"

"Mmmm?"

I had another question, but I wasn't sure I wanted to ask it. I thought it might be in that category of things that kids know and adults know, but each side pretends the other doesn't know, because it just makes everyone uncomfortable. I decided to risk it.

"Does Mr. Sherwood hit his wife? Does he, like, beat up on her? Does he beat up on Robert?"

My dad straightened up and looked at me, scrunching his eyebrows together. "Who told you that?"

Well, I wasn't going to confess to eavesdropping when I hadn't even served my sentence for disappearing, so I said,

"Oh, nobody. I hear him yelling sometimes. I just wondered." I hoped that would be explanation enough.

My dad looked over at my mom, who was listening from Charlie's bed. When I'd asked the question about Robert's dad, Charlie had popped up like a marionette springing to life. His eyes were round, his attention suddenly riveted.

I could tell that Mom was uneasy about the direction our conversation was going. She looked nervously from me to Dad to Charlie and back to Dad. Then she stood up, brushed her skirt smooth, and said, "You know, I think we've talked about Robert's dad just about enough for one night. I think it's about time you two squirts went to sleep. We can talk in the morning. Goodnight, Sport." She kissed Charlie on the cheek and gave him a little push back down onto his pillow.

"Good night, Pumpkin." She gave me a hug and a kiss, and Dad hugged and kissed us both, and they went quietly out and down the stairs. Charlie and I knew they were going to be talking about the issue of what to tell us about Robert's dad. They kept quiet until they were halfway down the stairs, and then their voices started up.

We lay there in the streetlamp's glow in our little room for a minute, and then Charlie propped himself up on one elbow and softly asked, "Lizzie, does Robert's dad do that? Hit people? Like hard? Even ladies?"

"I think so." (And I realized for the first time that I really did think so. It had a sobering effect.) "Maybe not Robert. But Mrs. Sherwood. I think so."

"How do you know? Did Robert tell you?"

"No, but I heard Mom and Dad talking about it. At least, I'm pretty sure that's what they were talking about. And think about it, Charlie. Sometimes we don't see Robert's mom for a long time. And when I go knock on the door, Robert answers and he says something like, 'Hang on. I'll go get my jacket,' and then he comes out. And one time she had a big black and blue mark across her cheek and her nose, and she said she bumped into the closet door. But now I wonder."

Charlie lay back down, his hands behind his head in thinking position. "Gee," he said. "That's awful."

"Yeah," I agreed. "Poor Robert. Poor Robert's mom."

We were both lying on our backs, staring thoughtfully at the ceiling, sorting out these foreign, disturbing speculations. But after a little while, the peace of our little room, the quiet of the summer evening, the faint murmur of our parents' voices downstairs…these combined to lull us into drowsiness. After all, Charlie and I were safe in our citadel, no matter what dark forces were operating next door. I heard Charlie's breathing slow and deepen, and then I was asleep.

CHAPTER TWENTY

The next day was Saturday. When I first woke up I was a little disoriented. I had been anticipating my birthday for so long that it was a jolt switching to post-birthday mode. And there was the added adjustment of realizing that my birthday had come and gone, and I was still without a hunting knife. Granted, I did now own a bicycle, which I couldn't ride for a week, but I was still knifeless and, it seemed, likely to remain so. The thought of Robert and all his troubles crossed my mind as well, but I felt helpless to deal with them, so I pushed them from my mind and fell to concentrating on my own situation.

Charlie was still asleep, so I slipped quietly from my bed and padded downstairs to the kitchen. My parents were sitting at the breakfast table, and it was obvious they'd been talking about me, because they stopped talking the minute I stepped through the kitchen door. There was an awkward little silence, which my mom tried to fill, saying brightly, "So! How's it feel to be eight?"

Mildly irritated by that obvious subterfuge, I sighed, "Fine," and climbed into my chair. There was another uncomfortable moment, and my parents' eyes met, exchanging some kind of telegraphic message. Then my mother took a deep breath, folded her hands on the table, and began.

"Lizzie, do you remember last night? You remember you asked us about Robert's dad? Well, Daddy and I have talked about it. We're not sure what to tell...how much you can understand. We don't want you to worry. We sure don't want you to be scared. Besides that, we care about Robert's feelings, and we want to respect his mom's privacy. So before we even talk about any of this, we need you to promise to keep it just in our family. Do you think you can promise that?"

My mind went reeling back to the previous day, when Robert had extracted just such a promise from me on the front porch. My parents had discovered Robert's secret before I told them, but now I was being entrusted with more private confidences. Was this what being eight was going to be like?

"Well, okay, but are you telling Charlie?" I asked.

My parents exchanged another eye telegram. My mom seemed a little desperate this time.

"Oh, I don't know, Honey. He's only six. I guess so. I'm not sure we can ask you to keep a secret from your own brother."

I was relieved about that. Charlie was pretty easy-going, but he could be persistent. And we did share a room. There was something about the camaraderie of a dark and cozy bedroom that encouraged the sharing of secrets.

My dad was continuing, choosing his words carefully. "You know, Lizzie, that Robert's dad sometimes has too much to drink. Too much alcohol. Drinks that have alcohol in them. Like beer, or whiskey, or wine. And when people drink too much alcohol, they just...do things...things they wouldn't do otherwise. Alcohol can make your brain not think very well."

"But Robert's dad is mean...well, mean or fake nice...even when he hasn't been drinking!" I was trying to sort out where the guilt lay.

"Well, I'm not sure we can always tell when he's been drinking. But, you're right. He does have a mean streak. And he has a pretty bad temper. So, when you put all that in the mixer—a mean man with a bad temper who drinks too much—well, you get a guy who sometimes loses control. Sometimes he might even hit somebody smaller and weaker, like Robert's mom. I gotta tell you, though, Honey, I don't think he hits your friend. I don't think they could hide that."

My mom chimed in. "Lizzie, Robert's mom is probably very…embarrassed about it, about her husband. I don't think she and Robert want anyone to know about all this trouble."

There was clearly a parental threat in Mom's voice, and I promised, "Okay, I won't tell, but are you sure about…I mean, it doesn't seem like Robert's *safe* over there."

Mom responded hurriedly, "Oh, no, Lizzie. We really think Robert's okay in his house. But I'm sure he feels terrible if his father hurts his mother. Robert is probably really the only good friend she's got."

That seemed so odd to me, so out of the natural order, that a child should have to be the supply of friendship for his parent. But I realized I couldn't remember a time when I'd seen Mrs. Sherwood leaving her house looking dressed up and happy. I'd never seen her sitting on her porch steps with a neighbor, chattering away or laughing together. I thought about all the times I'd seen my own mother with her friends. I'd taken it for granted that mothers talked on the phone, traded recipes over the fence, planned picnics with other families. I'd seen my mom with her friends, laughing so hard that tears rolled down their cheeks and they gasped for breath.

So…Robert's mom was friendless. "Gee, Mom, maybe you could share some of your friends. Maybe she could be in one of your clubs, you know, like that Thirty-seven Club."

My parents were in a bridge club, but that was for couples, and I couldn't picture Mr. Sherwood dressing up in a suit and going out to sit at a card table to play cards with a bunch of other couples. The Thirty-seven Club, on the other hand, had only women members. Back in 1937, a group of thirty-seven ladies of St. Luke had formed a social club that met for programs and refreshments and conversation. I wasn't sure if there always had to be exactly thirty-seven members, but I knew members came and went, because my own mother told me she had joined in 1945, the year I was born. I reasoned that if Mrs. Sherwood could become a member of that group, she'd automatically have thirty-six new friends.

Something about my suggestion, however, seemed to make my mother uncomfortable, or even a little embarrassed. "Well," she started hesitantly, "I guess I could get the club to invite her, and maybe I will, but I'm not sure it'd be such a good idea. And I think she'd say no, anyway. It's hard to explain."

Mom looked from Dad to me and back to Dad. My father seemed amused, and he raised his eyebrows and cocked his head, inviting the explanation. I could tell my mother was exasperated with him, but my presence kept her on the hook.

"The thing is, Honey, we're all kind of...well, kind of...we all have a lot in common. We're all sort of the same, in some ways, so we all feel really comfortable with each other. Like, we all went to college." She thought a minute, tapping one finger on the table. "No, I guess Bonnie and Anne didn't. Oh, I don't know. I'm not trying to leave her out, Sweetie, but I just can't imagine her having all of us over to her house, even if Robert's dad weren't there. Oh, stop looking at me that way, Mister! Can you picture it? Honestly?"

My dad was looking at Mom with an expression that clearly showed he was enjoying her discomfort. Mom floundered on, "Oh, all right, I'll bring her name up. But I can't very well explain her situation, can I? And I still think she'll say no."

"Well, maybe she'd just like to be invited," Dad offered by way of a truce.

"In my class, we can't have a club that doesn't have everyone in it," I observed. "Otherwise, it makes people feel left out."

My parents looked at me. There was a short silence. Then Daddy said, "The public school. A better world. The front lines of democracy."

I had no idea what he was talking about, but I could feel the shift in the conversation, and I knew my parents were somehow pleased with me.

At that point we heard Charlie thudding down the stairs. He came into the kitchen, climbed into his chair, and looked curiously at the three of us basking in an unusual pool of quiet.

Mom inhaled and began, "Charlie, before you eat, we have something we need to talk about."

Charlie sighed. "I know. It's about Robert's dad. He drinks too much. He hits Robert's mom. What a meanie. Someone should beat *him* up! Do you think you could beat him up, Dad?"

Mom and Dad exchanged a surprised glance. After a startled little silence, Dad answered, "Well, I guess I might be able to, but I'd get in trouble for it."

"Mr. Sherwood should get in trouble even more, then. He's bigger than her. Pass the Wheaties."

My parents seemed reluctant to lose control of the conversation, but I found Charlie's simple equation of justice comforting, and his matter-of-factness seemed to clear the air. Absentmindedly, Dad pushed the Wheaties box over to Charlie, who poured himself a bowlful, added milk and a heap of sugar, and started eating. He looked back and forth from Mom to Dad a couple times to check if there was any more information coming. Satisfied that the discussion had ended, he adjusted the Wheaties box to reading range and continued slurping down his cereal.

I watched him for a minute. I had once heard Grace refer to someone as "an odd little duck," and the phrase popped into my mind. Charlie was an odd little duck. Nice, but odd. Our parents were watching him, too. Finally, Mom said, "Charlie, it's a secret. About the hitting. We don't want to embarrass them. This is important, Charlie."

"*Embarrass* them? It's not *embarrassing*! It's *awful*! If somebody was beating me up all the time, I'd call the cops!"

"Yeah, why don't they just call the cops?" I chimed in.

My poor parents. It was starting to wear on them, explaining shades of gray to their black-and-white kids. Mom tried. "Kids, in a little town like this, everybody knows everybody else's business. If the police come to your house, then everyone wants to know why. Everyone talks about it. Some people would say mean things, even about Robert's mom. And I'm not sure what the police can do anyway. Robert's mom would have to ask them to arrest her own husband. Even if he went to jail for the night, when he got home, he'd be madder than ever."

My mother's voice wound down. Her explanation seemed to have brought home the hopelessness of it all. "It's all just a really depressing situation, kids. We'll just try to be good friends when they need us."

Breakfast seemed sad after that. We ate quietly, all of us thinking about the worrisome circumstances next door. It was my first experience with something that couldn't be fixed.

CHAPTER TWENTY-ONE

When we finished eating, the routine of our Saturday mornings reasserted itself. Dad went out to the garage to sharpen the lawn mower. Mom drove off in the station wagon to buy groceries at Jack's. Charlie meandered away down the alley, looking for somebody to play with. I felt restless and vaguely uneasy, but I just sat there at the kitchen table, thinking back over all the events of the previous day.

I got to thinking about my hunting knife, the one I'd failed to receive. I wandered out to the front room, where the Outdoorsman catalog was still lying on the end table. I flipped it open to the worn, dog-eared page with the picture of my knife, the sheath, and the strap that held everything in place. Somewhere in the back of my mind, an idea began to put itself together. I went back into the kitchen. No one was around, and it was quiet in the house. From outside came a metallic, scraping noise as my father sharpened the mower blades.

Feeling self-conscious but a little excited, I walked to the silverware drawer and slid it open. Guiltily, I rifled through the drawer. There were several sharp knives: five or six steak knives, a fat knife Mom used for chopping, a carving knife, and a small paring knife. I took out the paring knife and looked it over. It was worn from much use, and the blade was only about four inches long, but I thought it had potential. I looked around the kitchen. I peered out the screen door, checking to make sure my dad was still fussing over the mower.

Feeling more excitement than guilt, I carried Mom's paring knife up the stairs and into my room. I laid it down on my bed and stood staring speculatively at it. I needed a case. The sheath in the catalog was leather, but I didn't have any pieces of leather around. But wait. Was a chamois made of leather? I ran down the stairs, out the front door, and around to the garage. Sorting through the bin of car-washing stuff under my dad's workbench, I found a square of chamois cloth that had stiffened into a wadded-up ball. I took it back upstairs and soaked it with water in the bathroom sink. When it softened up, I squeezed out the extra water and then plastered it down flat on the linoleum floor.

Retrieving the paring knife from the bedroom, I laid it down on the damp chamois and considered how to proceed. The simplest plan seemed to be to just fold the chamois cloth over the blade of the knife, and maybe over some of the handle, and then cut the cloth to fit.

I was tired of running downstairs and increasingly edgy about getting caught, so I used the bandage scissors from the medicine cabinet to do the trimming. When that was done, I was pretty satisfied with the emerging little case for my knife, but the open side of the fold needed to be fastened together somehow. I considered sewing it, but the whole process of finding the right needle and thread and then figuring out how and where to sew just seemed insurmountable. I thought about glue, but I didn't know how I could manage to glue just the right amount along the inner edge, and I doubted whether it would hold, anyway.

Then I noticed the bandage scissors on the floor, and they reminded me of the fat roll of adhesive tape I'd seen in the medicine cabinet. I got it down and pulled off about a foot of the heavy white canvas tape. It was pretty unwieldy, and I had a lot of trouble trying to stick it on the wet chamois. After a few frustrating minutes, I wadded the tape into a ball and threw it in the wastebasket. I decided to hang the damp chamois by the open window to dry while I tackled the problem of attaching the homemade sheath to my leg. I tried several belts, both Charlie's and my own, wrapping them around my right shin several times and then trying to buckle them, but they just wouldn't buckle snuggly. I rejected the solution of tying the sheath to my leg with twine, since that would entail tying and untying every time.

I really needed something elastic that would buckle or clip somehow. My suspenders! I ran back to my room and found the suspenders still hooked to the pants I'd worn the day before. I unhooked them and studied their construction a minute or so. Sitting down on the bedroom floor, I fiddled around with the elastic straps, wrapping them around my leg several different ways before finally finding a way to clip them back on themselves. I stood up, holding my pajama pant leg up to study the effect. It wasn't perfect—the suspenders were a little bunchy and cumbersome—but I was pretty sure they'd hold my knife in place. I'd need to wear long pants.

I went back to the bathroom, took the slightly drier piece of chamois out of the window, and re-fashioned my sheath. Cutting a new length of adhesive tape, I tried a new tack—taping along the length of the fold and then wrapping several shorter lengths around the sheath as reinforcement. Everything seemed to be holding.

Next I tried slipping the paring knife into its case. It seemed to fit fine, and I felt a little thrill of accomplishment. Standing up, I stuffed the knife-and-sheath arrangement down between the suspender straps and my leg. I stood carefully back up. I was pretty excited at that point. My pajama pant leg slipped down and covered everything.

Gingerly, I took a few steps. The suspenders pulled a little, but they stayed fastened. I could feel the paring knife snug and tight against the outside of my leg. It was a grand secret thing, and I strutted around with increasing confidence and growing excitement.

I gathered up all the stuff I'd strewn about during the construction process, putting the roll of tape and the scissors back in the medicine cabinet and throwing the unused scraps of tape and chamois cloth into the bathroom wastebasket. It never occurred to me that my mom might find the contents of the bin somewhat of a puzzle. The bathroom looked okay now, so I decided to get dressed and get started on my day.

I took my pajamas off and pulled on my favorite pair of hand-me-down jeans. They were a little loose, but I decided against a belt. I was afraid that if my mom noticed me wearing a belt, she'd ask why I wasn't wearing my new suspenders. I wasn't prepared to explain.

The house still felt quiet and empty, so I went softly down the hall to check myself out in the full-length mirror. Surveying my reflection carefully, I speculated that a critical observer might notice a slightly rumpled look to the right leg of my jeans, but I couldn't think of anyone who would be interested enough to look closely.

I inched my pant leg up to see if everything was still in place. I admitted to myself that I hadn't quite achieved the rugged cowboy image suggested by the picture in the

Outdoorsman catalog, but still, when my pant leg was down, I thought I looked pretty good. I was reasonably satisfied. It was time to show Robert.

CHAPTER TWENTY-TWO

I went through the kitchen and out onto the back porch. Remembering how Robert's dad had hauled him away from my birthday party, I wasn't sure it was wise to just go banging on their back door. Then I noticed that their garage door was open, and their car was gone. That meant Robert's dad wasn't home, and even if the whole family was gone, I could knock on their door without worrying about getting Robert in trouble.

I climbed their back porch steps, and then I knew Robert was home, because I could hear him talking to his mom. Robert's voice asked, "But what do you think it might be?"

His mom answered, "I don't know, Honey, but he seemed pretty excited about it." I could tell she was smiling, which in itself was pretty unusual, and definitely a good omen for me.

I knocked on the screen door, and Robert appeared.

"Hi, Lizzie. Hey, what'd you get for your big present?"

At that point I realized that Robert hadn't heard about my bicycle, or my falling asleep in the cave, or the drowning bell, or anything.

"C'mon out. I got a lot to tell you," I said, and we sat down on his back steps in the morning sunshine, and I told him all about the end of my birthday.

Robert grew wide-eyed and silent. He was pretty impressed. He and I together had experienced so many imaginary adventures that it caught us both by surprise that one of us had had some excitement in real life.

"You wanna see my new bike?" I concluded.

"Sure, let's go before my dad gets back."

"Where'd he go?"

"We're not sure. Downtown, I think. He said he was gonna get me a present."

"Really? How come? I thought he was...well, you know, he was in sort of a bad mood."

"Yeah, I dunno. When I got up this morning he seemed sort of...like he was full of energy!" Robert demonstrated by throwing his arms out to the sides and flapping them around.

"Well, did you ask for something? Do you know what you're getting?"

"No." Robert looked down his long driveway towards the street. "I just hope it goes okay."

"How could a present not go okay?"

Robert shrugged. "Oh, you know. Like once my dad gave my mom a scale for weighing herself. He told her it was so she wouldn't get fat."

"Your mom's not fat," I observed.

Robert looked at me patiently. "No, she's not. It hurt her feelings." He looked back down the driveway. "She laughed, but it hurt her feelings. She weighs herself every day now."

I didn't know what to say then. I felt as though I had accidentally pried into Robert's family secrets.

Trying to get past the moment, I blurted, "C'mon. Help me get the garage door open."

Together we hoisted the heavy door up, and the morning light flooded into the dusty garage. There at the back stood my new bicycle, leaning on its silver kickstand, its blue fenders gleaming in contrast with the dark wood of the garage walls. It seemed almost alive, standing there waiting for me. It was as close as I could come to having a pony.

"Wow!" Robert stood in round-eyed awe. Our neighborhood wasn't poor, but still, few kids received brand new bicycles, and girls were less likely to get them than boys. Robert recovered himself and asked, "Can you ride it?"

"Well, *I can* ride it, but I *may not* ride it for one week," I grinned, mimicking my second-grade teacher's grammatical distinction.

"Oh, yeah, because of the drowning bell thing, right?"

"Yeah, but it's okay. I can wait a week."

Robert glanced at me for a moment, then looked away. In a voice conveying just the right combination of sympathy and nonchalance, he said, "Yeah, it's a beauty. Sorry about your knife, though."

"Hey, I forgot! That's what I came to show you! Look!" I tugged my pant leg up to reveal my suspender-girded shin.

Robert stared at my leg. He cocked his head, his forehead wrinkled in puzzlement. Then his face broke into a wide grin. "Hey! Neat! Does it really stay up?"

"So far. It kind of pokes me sometimes, though. I might need to just…kind of…maybe put it more on the side or something." I was bending over, tugging the elastic straps this way and that, when Robert and I caught sight of his father's car pulling into the driveway.

Mr. Sherwood slowed his car to a stop and climbed out. He seemed very pleased about something, and, as Robert had reported, full of energy. He opened the door to the back seat and pulled out a long, thin package wrapped in the characteristic green-and-gold striped paper from Sportsman's store.

"Hey, Robbie! C'mere! Look what your old man gotcha!"

I was stunned. I was so taken aback by Mr. Sherwood's behavior that I was frozen to the spot. I'd never heard Mr. Sherwood, or anyone, for that matter, call Robert "Robbie."

I'd never known him to give Robert a surprise of any kind. I'd never seen him so…jolly.

Robert seemed equally transfixed for a moment, and then he approached his dad cautiously. He was forcing a tentative smile, but I could tell he was nervously calculating what reaction to display.

"What is it, Dad?" His voice sounded small and uncertain.

"Well, open it up and see!" Robert's dad sounded almost gleeful, which left me totally confused. I was remembering how he'd just lost his job and how he'd hauled Robert home from my party the night before. (Was it really just the night before?)

Robert took the package and, glancing uneasily up at his dad, he tore off the striped wrapping. Inside was a baseball bat—a small one just the right size for kids our age.

"Wow! A bat! It's really a nice one, Dad! Thanks!" Robert held the bat in a batter's grip and swung it a few times, all the while watching to see what his father might expect him to do next.

"Go on in and get your baseball," his dad said. "I'll pitch you some."

Robert said, "Okay," in a thin, tight voice. I thought he sounded close to tears, but he trotted gamely off to find his baseball.

I remembered the only other time I'd witnessed Robert and his dad playing ball, so I guessed how worried Robert must have felt as he went running up the back porch steps. When he came back with the ball a minute later, he looked like it was taking all his self-control not to cry. I'm pretty sure he'd forgotten I was even there. I wondered if I should leave him to his humiliation, but I couldn't seem to stop watching.

Robert's dad stood over his son and showed him just how to hold the bat, how to swing it, how to plant his feet. Then he took the ball and walked about twenty feet away. He turned and faced Robert.

"Okay, now, take a few practice swings. Wiggle the bat. Feel where the bat is. And watch the ball!" Then he pitched out a gently underhanded throw, and Robert swung, and he *hit the ball!* His dad snagged it out of the air and uttered a little congratulatory whoop. "Attaboy! Nice hit! How 'bout another one?"

Another pitch, and another hit, and another! I guess they kept it up for a half hour, Mr. Sherwood trying out different speeds, crazy angles. Robert missed some, but he hit more than he missed, and his dad didn't get upset even when he missed. He just chattered regular baseball chatter like, "Nice try, Kiddo! Sorry...bad toss, my fault. Good cut, Buddy!" I felt like I was watching a dream.

I've thought about that little ball-playing session many, many times in the years that have passed since then, and every time I've wondered if it really happened the way I remembered. It isn't that I didn't think Robert would have been capable of hitting the ball over and over like that. It's just that being around his dad usually made him so nervous that he couldn't do anything well. Sometimes I think, in view of everything that was to happen later, that that one happy interlude was one of life's unexpected and bittersweet favors—evidence that there was goodness and affection buried in Robert's troubled relationship with his father.

Whatever the reason, Robert and his dad were playing ball together in the sunlight, having fun, a look of relaxed affection on their faces. I was so happy for Robert. And because I was eight, I just assumed that this was the happy ending…this was the way it would be between the two of them from that morning on.

After half an hour or so, Mr. Sherwood caught one last ball out of the air and said, "Whew! That's good for now, Buddy! Let's go see what Mom has for lunch." They went up their back steps together, Mr. Sherwood's hand resting easily on Robert's head. There was Mrs. Sherwood at the back door, smiling and drying her hands on her apron. It was just so *normal*.

I turned to go up my own back steps then and spotted my dad standing by the corner of the house, leaning on the lawn mower handle. "Did you see that, Daddy?" I asked.

"Yup." My dad was just standing there, nodding thoughtfully and staring over at the Sherwood house. "Yup," he repeated, shook his head, and then went with me up our own back steps for lunch.

CHAPTER TWENTY-THREE

I guess I was quieter than usual at the table. I was thinking about Robert, and about his dad, and about my knife, and about my bicycle standing unused in the garage. My mother must have been feeling a little sorry for me, because about halfway through her ham sandwich she said, "Okay. Who wants to go swimming this afternoon?"

That sounded good to me. I played with Robert nearly every day in the summer, but after watching my friend play ball with his father that morning, I felt hesitant about interrupting their time together. Losing Robert to his father was a new experience for me. I knew I should be happy for him, but I was left a little aimless and lonely.

Most of the swimming in St. Luke took place at the public beach not far from our dock. There was a strip of rock-strewn sand, and extending from the shore, a squared-off horseshoe of wooden pier that enclosed the younger kids' swimming area. Out beyond the horseshoe was an anchored raft where St. Luke's teenagers sunned themselves and showed off and horsed around. Up on the bank above the sand there were wide concrete steps where moms and a scattering of dads sat to watch their kids and chat and read magazines. There was a lifeguard in an elevated chair out on the horseshoe, but a hot July afternoon often drew two or three hundred kids, and there was no way one lifeguard could watch everybody at once. So quite a few moms and dads came along to make sure their own small fry bobbed up periodically among the beach balls and swimming caps and inner tubes.

Charlie and I were among those kids who weren't allowed to swim without a parent along. Mom said the water was so murky that any kid who ducked down two inches under the water was invisible, and that so many kids were doing cannonballs off the dock that they were bound to land on submerged swimmers pretty much every time. Mom was pretty watchful when Charlie and I were in the water. We really didn't mind having Mom along. She didn't fuss at us in front of our friends, and it was good to have someone to admire our dead-man's float and keep an eye on our towels with the nickels tied into the corners. Once in a while Mom swam a little bit, but mostly she sat on the warm steps and talked and laughed with the friends she invariably met there.

Anyway, that Saturday when Mom asked if anyone wanted to go swimming, Charlie and I raced through lunch and went tearing up the stairs to change into our suits and find our towels. Usually when Charlie and I changed clothes in our room together, we just sort of turned our backs on each other, but that day Charlie must have glanced over at me, because suddenly he blurted out, "Hey! What's on your leg? Is that your suspenders?"

I was a little embarrassed. "Oh, yeah. See, it's a knife thing...a knife holder. Prob'bly...don't tell Mom, okay?"

"Is that Mom's paring knife?"

I sighed. "Yeah, so don't go blabbing to Mom, okay? I'll put it back."

"Well, geez, Lizzie, you better! Mom uses that knife all the time. She's gonna miss it."

"Okay, okay. I'll put it back tomorrow."

Charlie went back to changing his clothes, but he was shaking his head back and forth. As he pulled his swimming suit string tight across his skinny little torso, he muttered, "Sometimes I can't believe you're the *oldest!*"

Suddenly aware of my knife as contraband, I put it, the chamois sheath, and the suspenders far back under my bed. I rubbed away at the suspender marks on my leg, hoping Mom wouldn't notice them. I thought about putting my jeans back on over my swimming suit but decided against it. Mom had picked out my suit and it had a row of ruffles around the hips, or where the hips would someday be. This was Mom's attempt to disguise my bony frame and convey the illusion of femininity. I was mildly contemptuous of the ruffles, and I found they bunched up into uncomfortable lumps if I tried to wear pants over them. I settled for wrapping myself in my big blue swimming towel, and then headed back downstairs with Charlie.

When we got out to the driveway, I looked over towards Robert's house, wondering where he was, wondering if he and his dad were still having fun together. Again I felt that unfamiliar pang of jealousy. What if Robert and his dad started spending lots of time together? Who would be my best friend?

I noticed that his dad's car was gone, and considered a moment whether I should run over and see if Robert was home, if he wanted to go swimming with us. But, at that moment, Mom came breezing out the back door, and I stopped worrying about my friend and climbed into the back of the car with my brother. Mom drove us the few blocks to the park by the swimming beach, and Charlie and I looked for our friends' cars lined up by the curb.

"Hey, there's Denny Fitzpatrick's car. They must be back from their grandma's."

"Yeah, and there's Krieger's new station wagon. I hope Maury brought the air mattresses!"

Mom gathered up her wide hat, her sunglasses, beach bag, and purse and headed off to the concrete steps. My dad, who'd been a Navy Seabee in the war, said he never could establish a beachhead like Mom did. Charlie and I trotted down the steps, tossing our towels in Mom's direction as we scanned the water for familiar heads amidst the splashy froth of kids, water toys, and waves.

Lake swimming is nothing like pool swimming, and people who've tried both know the difference. St. Luke Lake in July was warm and murky. The bottom of the lake was a mixture of silt and rocks, and lots of kids wore old sneakers in the water. If we were barefoot, we tried to put our feet down as seldom as possible, since doing so risked stepping on sharp rocks or having fine, silky mud squish up between your toes. The rocks hurt and the mud was disgusting. On hot summer afternoons, when hundreds of kids showed up, the churning of all those arms and legs raised the silt and kept the water perpetually cloudy. Most of us learned to tread water for long minutes at a time. When we did choose to walk through the chest-deep water, we adopted a kind of slow motion, high-bouncing step that propelled us along like languid ballet dancers. Years later, when I saw the grainy television images of astronauts walking on the moon, I recognized immediately the sensation of bounding through the water of St. Luke Lake.

When we needed a break from swimming, we'd climb out, dry off, and pry the nickels from the knots we'd tied in the corners of our towels. Standing in line at the candy counter, our bare feet made little "snick—snick" noises as they stuck to the warm popsicle-juice-covered cement.

In light of all that was to happen later that day, it seems odd to me that Charlie and I had such an ordinary, peaceful afternoon. I did think of Robert every now and then. I missed him when Charlie and I debated the merits of popsicles versus frozen candy bars, because Robert always agreed with me that the candy bars took longer to eat and were, therefore, a better value. I missed him when we were heading for the car with our towels tied like Superman capes around our necks. But most of the time, I just enjoyed myself, and when, in mid-afternoon, Charlie paused on the edge of the dock and observed, "We should've invited Robert," I responded, "Well, his dad's home." When I said that, Charlie looked at me oddly and added, "Yeah. I know."

I do remember feeling a little uneasy after Charlie made that comment. I guess he must have dissipated the optimistic fog I'd wrapped myself in after watching Robert with his dad that morning. The weekend's events had made me realize that Robert and I always looked forward to Monday together, knowing his dad would be absent from the house until Friday, giving us five days to play without tailoring our movements to Mr. Sherwood's mercurial temperament. Now I wondered how his temperament was weathering the afternoon.

Regardless of our concerns about Robert, we stayed at the lake long into the afternoon, taking treat breaks every hour or so and stretching out on our towels occasionally to rest in the sun.   Then about four-thirty or so, Mom stood up, stretched, and began packing up her beach bag with all her paraphernalia, and Charlie and I knew it was time to go.

CHAPTER TWENTY-FOUR

When we pulled into our driveway, I noticed that Mr. Sherwood's car was still gone. As we were piling out of our car, slamming the doors shut, and dragging our stuff across the yard, Robert emerged from his back door.

"Hi, you guys! I heard your car. I thought maybe it was my dad."

"Where is he anyway?" I asked.

"We don't know for sure." Robert stood on his back step, casting anxious glances toward the street as though he were expecting his father at any moment. Robert sounded small and worried. I wondered whether or not he was wishing for his father to appear. I thought, "Have things always been this way with Robert? Have I just not ever really noticed? Is it because I'm eight now? Will I start to notice all kinds of things that are wrong with the world?"

I knew one thing for sure. I was sorry we hadn't taken Robert swimming. He must have been in his house all afternoon, wondering where his father was and worrying every time a car went by. A wave of unfamiliar protectiveness swept over me. I called out, "Hey, Robert! That was some good hitting today. I didn't even know you could do that!"

Robert turned in my direction, struggling to tune in to what I'd said. Then he grinned a little and said, "Yeah! I think my dad was kind of surprised. Actually, I was kind of surprised myself!"

"Well, I gotta go change my clothes. You wanna play after that?"

"Sure. Okay. I'll wait on your steps." And just as he said that, just as he was plunking himself down on our porch step, we both caught sight of his father's car pulling into the long driveway. Robert jumped back up. He was flapping his arms nervously out at the sides and hopping on and off the bottom step. He seemed to be debating whether to stay put or to run to welcome his dad.

Mr. Sherwood climbed out of his car, waved a relaxed greeting in our direction, and turned to retrieve a brown paper grocery sack from the back seat. I could hear glass bottles clanking, a sound which held no meaning for me, but I noticed Robert's face puckering with concern.

Affecting nonchalance, he asked unsteadily, "Hey, whatcha got in the sack, Daddy?"

His father looked over at Robert, grinned widely, and held the sack in the air. "I'll tell you what, Slugger! I got a real Saturday night celebration in this sack! Celebrating my home run king here!"

Robert watched his dad stride off towards his house, swinging the grocery sack. Mr. Sherwood was whistling "Take Me Out to the Ballgame." Robert kept his gaze fixed on his back door, even after it had banged shut. After a minute or so, he sank slowly back down on the step and sat there, hands on his knees, staring at his house.

I felt uncomfortable and somewhat puzzled. Something was clearly troubling my friend, but I could see nothing obviously worrisome. Finally, I said, "Well, I'll run up and change, Robert. I'll be back in a sec."

"Okay," was his preoccupied response. His attention remained on the house next door.

I ran into the house and upstairs to change out of my wet bathing suit. Once in my room, I peeled my suit, ruffles and all, down to my ankles and deposited it in a damp roll on the floor. My clothes from the morning were still on my bed, so it only took me a minute to get dressed, but when I sat on the floor to put my shoes back on, I spotted my suspenders and the paring knife, still in its chamois case, in a little tangle under the bed. Realizing I'd have to put Mom's kitchen knife back in the morning, I decided to strap it back on my leg, just for one last time. It took a few minutes to get it all arranged as snugly as before, and by the time I got back down to the porch again, Robert was wandering aimlessly around our back yard, picking up sticks and tossing them down again. Every few seconds, he looked over towards his back door.

"Wanna play with my new gas station?"

Robert shrugged. "Sure. I guess. I'll go ask my mom how long til dinner." Robert trotted off to find his mom while I waited for him. After a bit he reappeared. "I can play, but I *have, have* to be home in a half hour. My mom's fixing a really nice dinner. It's all my dad's favorite stuff. So I really, really have to be home in a half hour."

"Okay. Don't worry. We'll watch our living room clock. We'll make sure you get home on time."

The half hour passed peacefully while we played in the quiet of the late summer afternoon. The breeze came in through the window screens, lifting the sheer white curtains away from the windows in shifting, rounded billows. The summer smells of grass and honeysuckle drifted in, and my old friends the dust motes reflected gold from the slanting sunlight.

Still, Robert kept a careful eye on the time, and after about twenty-five minutes he said, "I better go. I don't wanna be late. Mom's really trying to make this a nice dinner."

I didn't realize, of course, all the complicated reasons why Robert didn't want to be late, so I asked, "What are you having, anyway?"

ELIZABETH EDSON BLOCK

"Well, it's a special dinner. For my dad. To keep him...you know...cheered up. About the job and everything. I think it's fried chicken and corn on the cob and strawberry shortcake."

"I love fried chicken! Wish I could eat over!"

"Uh, I think this is just for our family. Sorry, Lizzie. I know I owe you a lot of dinners."

I was embarrassed. I hadn't really meant to invite myself over. It was just that family celebrations seemed to be a pretty rare event in the Sherwood house, and I was trying to show enthusiasm.

"Oh, I didn't really mean that, Robert. I just meant...have a nice dinner. It...it sounds like...a lot of fun."

I needn't have worried about Robert's reaction. He was already heading through our kitchen to the back door. Robert's arrivals and departures were often like that. His thoughts would travel home before his body did, and his attention would remain at home for a while after he'd arrived somewhere else. Sometimes you even had to put yourself in his line of vision and repeat his name a couple of times to get his attention.

I followed him out to the back porch and said, "Seeya tomorrow."

In my own kitchen Mom was starting dinner, mashing crackers, eggs, hamburger, and some other stuff in a bowl. I sat down on a kitchen chair, feeling the need for some reassuring familiarity.

"Is that meat loaf?"

"Yup. You want to help, Sugar Plum?"

"No, I guess not." Pause. "Robert's mom is making fried chicken and corn on the cob and strawberry shortcake."

My mom stopped kneading the hamburger mixture and looked out the window toward Robert's house. After a minute she shook her head and said, "Oh, that poor woman. Maybe all this will straighten him out." She went back to squeezing the mixture in the bowl. "Probably not." She sighed and shook her head again.

Our own family dinner that night was nothing out of the ordinary, which is to say, it was cheery, the food was good and plentiful, teasing was dished out and taken, and our parents carried on two conversations—one at our level and one at theirs. At one point, Dad said something that made Mom laugh so hard she had to go spit her food out in the sink. That happened about once a week. I'm sure my dad did it on purpose, almost as though he awarded himself a point every time it happened. That night, when my mom came back to the table, wiping tears from her eyes, I wondered how dinner was going at Robert's house. I was pretty sure Robert's mom wasn't having as much fun as mine, no matter how great the fried chicken turned out. I bet she'd never had to spit out her food in the sink.

Saturday night was game night at our house, so after the dishes were done, Charlie and I moved all my gas station stuff off the card table and set up the Parcheesi board. Our family played cutthroat Parcheesi. We had a family tradition called Ultimate Loser. In a game like Parcheesi, we played until somebody won, but then we continued to play until someone was second, third, and last. Whoever was last was the Ultimate Loser.

That might sound kind of mean to some people, but Charlie and I liked it. Even if someone else was the winner, it still gave you something to shoot for. Of course, if you were the Ultimate Loser, you wanted to play another game as soon as possible. Sometimes we played four or five games in a row. At some point on game night Mom usually made popcorn and Dad would open up four bottles of root beer or orange Nehi. During the winter we had a fire in the fireplace, and in the summer we kept a little tablet on the mantel, and we wrote down how late it was before we had to turn on the living room light. (That started out as Mom's idea of an educational experience, but it sort of evolved into a celebration of the long summer evenings.) That night we turned the lights on at 8:15, but it wasn't really dark out. I remember that time, because we later had to reconstruct the evening's events, and we estimated we'd finally put the Parcheesi board away about 8:45, based on the fact that we'd played one game with the light on. Mom was the Ultimate

Loser, so we got to quit playing. When Dad was the Ultimate Loser, we always had to play one more game.

After the Parcheesi game was back in the box, Mom glanced at the mantel clock and said, "You know, kids, I think Daddy and I will take some watermelon over to the Anderson's house. She's kind of cooped up with that new baby. He's got colic, and it's driving her crazy. Do you think you kids can get ready for bed by yourselves? We'll be back in fifteen minutes."

Charlie and I exchanged a look of suppressed delight. We were rarely left alone in the evening, even for a few minutes. The fact that the Anderson's house was just across the alley behind our house didn't lessen the fact that we would have the house to ourselves. Usually the bedtime routine involved Charlie and I dawdling a little over teeth brushing and book reading while Mom drifted around downstairs, picking up stuff, and Dad turned on the radio. After fifteen minutes or so, they'd climb the stairs to tuck us in and kiss us good night.

Having them out of the house meant that we could really stretch out our routine. We climbed the stairs together, and Charlie, in a quiet voice, said, "I'm gonna play with my Erector set. What are you gonna do?"

I had no particular plan, so when we reached our bedroom I sat on my bed and watched Charlie while he looked over the structure that Robert had been helping him with. "I wish Robert were here," he mused absentmindedly.

CHAPTER TWENTY-FIVE

That reminded me of Robert, and, once again, I wondered how his evening had gone. I went across the hall to the bathroom and stood on the edge of the bathtub to look out the high bathroom window at Robert's house next door. I caught a glimpse of my parents cutting across the back lawn on their way to the Anderson's. Looking back toward the Sherwood's house, though, there wasn't much to see from where I stood. There was a light on in Robert's kitchen, but I couldn't see anything except part of the kitchen counter. I needed a vantage point more directly across from the back part of their house.

Scrambling down from the rim of the bathtub, I walked down the hall and climbed the back stairs to the attic. Standing on my tiptoes, I craned my neck up and peeked out the octagon of clear glass in the center of the round window. I could see right down into Robert's kitchen.

Mr. Sherwood was standing in the middle of the room. He was holding Robert's baseball bat in one hand, and with his other hand he was holding his wife by her wrist. She seemed to be pulling away from him. Even though I couldn't hear them from where I stood in the darkening attic, it looked like Mr. Sherwood was yelling and his wife was crying. For a long moment I just stared, trying to reconcile what I was seeing with my own experience of reality. I just couldn't understand what could possibly be going on. Mr. Sherwood kept jerking on her wrist, and she kept trying to twist her arm away, and then she sort of kicked at him. That feeble attempt to resist must have set something off in him, because he put his face right up close to hers...I think he was shouting something...and then he lifted Robert's bat up high and brought it down twice on his wife's head.

My own head jerked back each time the bat came down. One blow must have caught her on the nose, because blood was spraying out even as she was dropping down to her knees. Mr. Sherwood hit her once more then. I couldn't see exactly where the bat struck, but Robert's mom sank down on the floor out of my sight.

The whole incident probably lasted only thirty seconds, and during that time I just watched in disbelief. I suppose I was waiting to wake up. And then I saw what seemed a flurry of blue fly across the lighted kitchen below and fling itself against Mr. Sherwood. Robert, looking hopelessly small in his blue pajamas, was banging his fists against his father and trying to grab the bat away. He was furiously kicking and punching at his dad, who responded in dazed irritation for a moment. Then he drew back his empty hand and gave Robert a tremendous swat, sending him flying on his backside across the kitchen floor. I saw my friend hit the wall and crumple over. Mr. Sherwood, still holding the bat, walked shakily towards his son. Robert was hunched against the wall, looking up in terror at his father.

I heard myself whisper, "Robert." My heart pumped once really hard. I felt a big "whomp" clear through my body. I was light-headed and totally without any coherent thought, but suddenly I was running. I tore down the two flights of stairs and ran back through the kitchen and out the back door. Racing across the lawn and up Robert's back steps, I hoped in desperation that Mr. Sherwood would somehow have disappeared. Through the screen I could see Robert sliding along the wall towards me. At first I didn't see his father, but then I heard a moaning sound. It was Mrs. Sherwood, still slumped on the floor. Robert's dad was standing over her, shaking the bat at her with one hand and drinking from a brown bottle that he held in the other hand. He looked like a different person than the man I'd seen playing with his son in the yard that day. I had no experience with either drunkenness or rage. To me, he just looked kind of sick and scary. His face was red and sweaty, his balance seemed unreliable, and he was rambling incoherently.

I froze outside the screen door for just a moment. Robert was still edging towards me, his back against the wall and his eyes on his father. Then he glanced toward the door and caught sight of me standing there. His eyes flew wide, and I yanked the screen open and yelled, "Robert! Run!"

Robert scrambled out the door, I grabbed his hand, and together we flew down the steps. Robert was pulling me in the direction of my house, but I realized with a shock of despair that my parents would not be there. "No, Robert! Nobody's home!" I yanked on his hand and pulled him down the driveway toward the front sidewalk. Robert's bare feet slapped against the cement. I heard the screen door bang, and then Mr. Sherwood was behind us. Robert looked over his shoulder, gave a little whimper, and stumbled momentarily. His dad lunged out at us and managed to grab the shoulder of his son's pajama shirt. Robert wriggled violently and pulled away, which seemed to enrage his father, who stumbled a little and swore in disgust.

Having no idea where safety lay, Robert and I turned and ran down the sidewalk towards the lake, which was two blocks away. Mr. Sherwood was running after us again, but his footsteps sounded heavy and unsteady. We were gaining a little distance, and by the end of the first block we were about twenty yards ahead.

As I ran I was dimly aware of something sharp poking me near my right ankle, and on some level I realized that my mom's knife was sliding down out of its suspender grip. I had let go of Robert's hand, but I was aware of Robert running just a step away from me, keeping up even though he was running barefoot. We flew across Second Street, not daring to look back, but when we reached the curb on the far side of the street, I heard Robert give a sharp cry. He must have tripped on the curb, and he fell full-length on the sidewalk, catching my feet from the side as he flung his hands out to break his fall. I crashed down in the grass by the sidewalk, and as I fell I felt the suspenders around my leg snap open. The elastic straps flipped apart, and the paring knife left its casing and skittered off into the grass.

Robert and I lay dazed for only a second, but as we recovered and struggled frantically to pick ourselves up, Mr. Sherwood caught up to us. He was closer to Robert than to me, and he swung the bat a little wildly in Robert's direction. Robert was on his feet by then, and he tried to step out of the way, covering his head with his hands, but the bat glanced off his elbow with a sharp cracking sound. He yelped in pain and tried to step backwards to get away, but his father caught him by the arm, yanking him back and forth like a cloth doll. Robert was crying and pleading, "Daddy, no, it's me, Robert! Don't, Daddy! Let me go!"

Then for a moment Mr. Sherwood lost his grip, and Robert fell away on the grass, rolling and scrambling to escape. Mr. Sherwood stepped toward him, raising the bat up over his head.

While Robert's dad had held his son's arm, I had just been crouching in the grass, immobilized by shock and fear. But as Mr. Sherwood lifted the bat in the air, I caught a glimpse of a shard of light in the grass a few inches from my hand. The blade of my mom's paring knife was reflecting off the glow from the streetlight. Without any thought or plan, I snatched up the knife and lunged at Robert's father. I had no real target in mind. Certainly I wasn't thinking about how to inflict real damage. I just reached out and stabbed him in the back of his thigh, which, I suppose, was the part of him closest to me. It was a strange feeling when the knife went into his leg—like sticking a knife into a grapefruit.

Mr. Sherwood froze in bewildered surprise for a moment. Then he roared out in pain, grabbed ineffectually at his thigh, and jerked his hand away in confusion when he felt the knife still stuck in his leg. Robert tried to run past him back in the direction of our houses, but his father spread his arms wide, the bat extending from his right hand, and Robert turned frantically away from him and headed back towards the lake. I didn't know what to do, so I just ran after Robert.

In the days that followed that long and terrible evening, a few insensitive people asked me why we didn't run to someone's house, or why we didn't yell for help. The truth is

I don't remember thinking much of anything during that wild chase down the sidewalk. But I remember seeing a mouse once, trapped in a corner of our basement, desperately running first one way, then another, even straight up the wall. That's what it was like for us. We just wanted to get far away from Mr. Sherwood.

I don't remember hollering or screaming, either, but, as it happened, someone did hear something. Grace had come out on her front porch to set out her empty milk bottles, and she heard what she said sounded like a cat fight from across the street and a few houses down toward the lake. She stepped on down to her front sidewalk and looked in the direction of the sounds. She thought she saw a couple of kids running like crazy in the direction of the lake, and a second later, she thought she made out the figure of a man loping unsteadily after the two children. She thought he was limping.

Of course, all this odd behavior disturbed her, so she hurried over to ring the doorbell at my house. The bell was answered, after a minute or two, by my brother Charlie, who was wondering where his big sister had gotten off to. A minute later, my parents came home by the back door to find a bewildered Charlie and an increasingly alarmed neighbor. Grace's anxious description of what she had witnessed confused and frightened my parents, and when they questioned the somewhat defensive Charlie, all he could offer was, "I don't know. I guess I heard her running down the stairs. I think…I might have heard her go out the back door."

That galvanized them into action. My dad ordered Charlie to wait in the house. He sent my mom and Grace to Robert's house to see if I was just over there playing, and he himself went off in a sprint down the sidewalk where Grace had seen two kids running toward the lake.

My mother told me later that the next hour or two passed like a nightmare for her. When she and Grace went around to the Sherwood's kitchen door, they discovered Robert's mother struggling to get up off the floor. There was blood all down the side of her face, and Mom could see that her lip and eye were discolored and swollen.

When Mrs. Sherwood saw her neighbors coming across the kitchen to help her, she looked frantically around for her husband and son. "Oh, no," she said. "Oh, no, Paul's gone after Robert. He's got that baseball bat. Oh, no, Marian, he's drunk. He's not in his right mind."

My mother felt physically sick when she heard that, but she felt she had to be calm for the frantic and beaten Mrs. Sherwood. "It'll be okay, Inez. Bob's gone after them. I think Lizzie's with Robert. We're calling an ambulance for you, but first we're calling the police, just in case."

Robert's mom protested that she was fine, that she wanted to try to find Robert, but my mother was adamant.

She called the police, the ambulance, and then she took Grace aside and said, "Get some neighbors. Get anybody. And take some flashlights. The kids might be on the Indian trails. Lizzie and Robert have a hiding place somewhere down there. I'll put Inez in the ambulance, and then I need to get Charlie. I'll come in the car." Mom and Grace gave each other a desperate hug, and Grace was out the door.

CHAPTER TWENTY-SIX

My mother had guessed right. When Robert and I crossed Lake Avenue and reached the park fronting the lake, we flew along the grassy bank, pelted down the wooden steps by our dock, and scrambled the few feet along the trails to our cave. Mr. Sherwood's injured leg, combined with his drunken instability, must have slowed him down. By the time we'd crossed into the park, the sound of his lumbering footsteps had receded a little.

Robert and I crammed ourselves into our hiding place as far as we could, and then we just sat there, our arms around each other, our eyes fixed on the open front of our cave. My heart was pounding so hard I could feel it in my throat and in my stomach. We were both trying to breathe in great gulps of air without making any noise. Robert was shaking and silently crying.

Then we heard the sound of heavy footsteps coming down the wooden stairs about ten feet from our hiding place. "Robert!" Mr. Sherwood's voice, angry and ragged, seemed to originate from right outside the cave. Robert and I shut our eyes and tightened ourselves into the smallest shapes possible.

"Robert! You come back here, you little rat bastard!" Mr. Sherwood continued unevenly down the steps, calling out Robert's name and making threats and cursing as he went. When he reached the bottom stair, he hesitated. Then we could hear him walk out on the dock a few steps and stop. He called out Robert's name again, and then we heard soft splashing sounds as he stepped down off the dock and into the shallow water along the shore. We could hear him slogging along in the water, his feet making irregular splashing sounds when he stumbled over rocks. As he came closer, we could see his dark outline against the water. The scrubby branches along the bank obscured his silhouette, but still, it seemed that if he just looked in our direction, he'd see us huddled there in the bank. As he stepped into our direct line of sight, he suddenly shouted, "I know you're here, Robert! You might as well come out!" There was a pause, and then, in a voice that seemed at once desperate and defeated, Mr. Sherwood cried out, "Dammit, Robert, you come *home* now!" There was an explosive cracking sound as Robert's father swung the bat down hard on a rock. The bat splintered apart, and some little pointed chip of it shot up and hit my knee.

That was when the terror just swept down over me. I felt something warm spreading up from where I was sitting. At first I thought I was bleeding from some unfelt wound, but then I realized I'd wet my pants. Even in that extreme circumstance, the shock and shame of wetting myself snapped me back to a measure of conscious thought and self-control.

We could hear small splashing sounds again as Mr. Sherwood waded on past us. He was still hollering, and each time he stumbled, we could hear him curse. The sounds receded as he made his way slowly down the shoreline away from us. Then we heard a couple of louder sounds—a sharp cry of pain, followed by a splash and another sound, like a melon dropping on the sidewalk.

Robert and I strained to hear more, but everything was eerily quiet. I was terrified that Mr. Sherwood was out there on the trail, sneaking up on us. Too frightened to move, we just sat there, tears slipping quietly down both our faces as we listened to the enormous silence.

Then suddenly out of that breathless stillness came a totally unexpected sound: the clear, insistent clang of the drowning bell. At the first hollow "bong" of the bell, Robert and I jerked in surprise and fear. So intent were we on trying to be absolutely quiet that my first reaction was to wish frantically that the bell would stop ringing. After a minute went by, though, the continuous bell sounds began to take hold of me. I didn't know who was ringing it, but I knew that whoever it was, it was a friend and a protector.

I squeezed my eyes shut for a second, and I took one deep breath and held it. Then, grabbing Robert's hand, I whispered fiercely, "Let's go!"

I didn't give Robert any time to hesitate. I just scrambled out of the cave, pulling my friend behind me. We tumbled forward onto the Indian trail, too scared to look around for Robert's dad. We just pounded blindly up the wooden steps to the bank and ran toward the sound of the bell.

And then the night must have filled with sounds. First there was the distant siren of the ambulance as it neared Robert's house. Two police cars, red lights spinning and sirens screaming, came racing down Lake Avenue from opposite directions toward the park. Voices emerged out of the late dusk as neighbors responded for the second time in as many days to the summons of the drowning bell. Flashlight beams danced over the grass like fireflies, and the bell kept ringing....

At the time, all of the sounds except the bell were lost on me. I was too overcome with fear to have the presence of mind to sort friendly sounds from unfriendly ones. Only the peal of the bell held my focus. The bell was where someone would catch me up and save me and save Robert, and we could be just two children again, and strong and kindly grownups would be in control.

And then we saw the platform, and on it, still straining away at the big wooden bell handle, was dear, dear Grace. Robert and I scrambled up beside her, threw our arms around her, and buried our faces against her. Our sobs broke out in earnest, and Grace held us close and let us cry.

Then other voices began to creep into the edges of my awareness, and I saw the criss-crossing flashlight beams coming toward us. Chief Galsworthy was striding across the grass, his face unfamiliar and stern in the flickering light. He spoke to the gathering knot of bewildered neighbors. "Okay, folks, Paul Sherwood is down here somewhere. He's drunk, and he's mad, and he's got a baseball bat. You can help us find him, but stay in pairs, and if you think you see him, don't try to approach him. Just give a shout. Keep him in your flashlight beam if you can."

Solemnly, people began to pair off and drift away through the scattered trees along the banks. I could tell they were nervous about coming face to face with Mr. Sherwood, because they trained their flashlights around for long moments before they moved ahead.

Chief Galsworthy left a couple of neighbors behind to watch over Grace and her two badly shaken charges, and then he aimed his own flashlight in the direction we'd come from, and he started off down the shoreline. That was when I heard someone urgently shouting my name, and I turned to see my father bounding up the concrete steps overlooking the swimming dock. When he caught sight of Robert and me, still clinging to Grace, he stopped still for just a second, then ran to us, dropped to his knees, and caught all three of us— me, Robert, and Grace—in the circle of his arms.

"Oh, Lizzie, my own baby girl! Thank God!" That was a lot of emotion from my even-tempered father, and his relief reinforced the sensation that Robert and I had been in real danger, but that now, with my father there, we were truly safe. My tears started anew, and I left Grace's side for the greater comfort of my father.

After a long hug, my dad leaned back, held me at arm's length, and asked, "Are you okay? Did he catch you? Did he hurt you?"

"Well," I had to think back. "He caught up once on the sidewalk, but we...I...we got away." I had just remembered about the knife, and about my stabbing Mr. Sherwood, and I wasn't sure how the usual rules of my well-mannered little universe applied. Ordinarily, of course, stabbing anyone would have been unthinkable, but I knew enough to credit the extremity of the circumstances. For the moment, I elected to continue my story without elaboration. "Then we ran down the steps by our dock, and down the trail, and then we hid in our cave. We heard Mr. Sherwood yelling and splashing around, and then...." And at that moment I looked over and caught sight of Robert's face.

In Robert's ashen and defeated expression, I read what had happened next. After all the shouting and splashing, we had heard a loud yelp and a big splash, and then we had heard nothing at all.

"Daddy, I think Mr. Sherwood...," I began, but my dad glanced at Robert, and he gripped my arms a little harder and looked at me intently and said, "We'll find him, Honey. All these people will help look for him. We'll find him." I knew the words were really directed at Robert, not at me.

But my father hadn't been there. He didn't know about the sudden quiet in the water. I exchanged glances with Robert. He was standing quietly, his arms at his sides. He looked at me with an old person's eyes, and then he turned his head and stared out into the darkness over the lake. Without altering his gaze, he said softly, "I think my dad fell down in the water by your dock." He paused. "I think he might be...hurt." There was another pause, and then Robert turned to my father. "My mom's hurt, too. She's in our kitchen."

My dad's voice was very calm, very gentle. "Your mom's going to be fine, Robert. Lizzie's mom is gathering up Charlie from our house, and then she's staying with your mom until the doctor comes. She'll be fine."

Even as my dad was reassuring Robert, I heard two car doors slam, and I looked over to see my mother and brother running toward us across the grass. My father rose quickly and went to meet them. I could hear my mom's voice, pitched high with fear and anxiety, but my dad took her by the shoulders and spoke to her in a low, measured tone. I could see Charlie looking up at Dad, then over at Robert and me. I was pretty sure my father was explaining the situation to my mother and telling her not to say anything that might upset Robert.

The rest of the time in the park that night was kind of unreal. There were flashlights flickering all around us by then, and voices calling out to each other through the darkness. Then there were louder, more urgent shouts coming from the direction of our dock. Chief Galsworthy emerged from the darkness and went off to speak with two men who were hurrying in our direction. Their voices weren't loud, but I could hear the concern and uncertainty. The small knot of people around the chief kept glancing in our direction and then quickly looking away.

My friend Robert actually seemed to grow smaller as he stood there, retreating somewhere deep within himself. He wasn't crying anymore. In fact, he made no sound at all. He was rocking slowly back and forth, then side to side, then back and forth again. Sometimes he would close his eyes hard for a second, but mostly he just stared blankly at the ground a little distance from his feet.

When Chief Galsworthy finished talking to the two men, he walked towards us, motioning for my dad to come closer. My father gave Robert and me a quick squeeze of reassurance, then went a few steps away to listen to the chief. I saw my dad put his hand up to his forehead and close his eyes, and I heard him say something, but I couldn't hear what it was. The two men stood there a minute, and the chief put his hand on Dad's shoulder and said something. I could hear the words "Robert" and "wife."

Dad came back to us then and got down on one knee in front of Robert. "Your mom is at the hospital, Robert, but she's going to be fine. They found your dad, and they're taking him to the hospital, too. He fell in the water and hit his head on a rock. We're going to take care of you until, well, until one of your parents can come home." My dad stood up, his hands still on Robert's shoulders. Turning to our neighbor, Dad said, "Grace, can you stay with Robert at his house until we find out when his mom...when one of his parents...can come home?"

Grace bent down and embraced Robert and said, a little too briskly, "Of course! Let's get you home, Sweetie. Oh, look, you don't even have any shoes on, for heaven's sake!"

Grace took Robert's hand and tugged him gently toward our station wagon. Robert let himself be led without protest.

My mom was looking over my head at my dad, and I saw him drop his eyes and shake his head just the slightest bit. I felt like I had just taken a big drink of something really cold. My mom closed her eyes hard for a second, and then she said, "I think Grace has the right idea. The station wagon will hold us all. We'll be nice and cozy, all together. Come on, kids."

We all filed across the grass to our car. I sat in front between Mom and Dad, and Grace sat in the middle seat between Robert and Charlie. None of us kids seemed to want to be in the back seat that night. Grace put her arm around Robert and pulled him over close beside her. For once, Charlie was quiet.

When we got home, we all climbed silently out of the car. Grace, her arm still around Robert, was walking him gently in the direction of his house. As I watched his small, pajama-clad form trailing away from me, I wanted desperately to help him somehow, to say something cheering or encouraging. "G'nite, Robert!" I finally called out. "I'm sure your folks will be back home tomorrow."

Robert stopped walking. Without even turning around, without lifting his head, he said quietly, "I don't think so. I think my dad's dead. I think he drowned in the lake." Then he continued walking. Grace put her hand up to her face, then hurried after Robert. They disappeared quietly into

Robert's darkened kitchen. A moment later, we saw his kitchen light go on.

Shocked and confused, I looked up at my parents' faces. Had I said something wrong? Was Robert right about his father? How did he know for sure?

My mother's eyes were shining with tears. She shook her head, looking down at me with infinite love and sadness. "Chief Galsworthy says Robert's daddy is gone, Honey. It was an accident."

My dad added, "You kids did just the right things, Lizzie. You kept yourselves safe and then you ran to find help. You did all the right things." He paused a moment, looking over toward Robert's house. "You've always been a good friend to Robert. Now we'll all be good friends to Robert and his mom."

And then, for the second night in a row, my father picked me up and carried me into our house and up the stairs to the sanctuary of our small bedroom. If he noticed that my trousers were still slightly wet, he said nothing.

CHAPTER TWENTY-SEVEN

Charlie and I changed into our pajamas. Mom took away my damp jeans and underwear without commenting. As I was pulling my pajama pants on, I noticed the faint impression the elastic suspenders had left on my leg. Only then did I realize that my mom's paring knife, along with my suspenders, was lying somewhere out there in the grass beside the sidewalk. The memory of my struggle with Mr. Sherwood overwhelmed me.

"I stabbed him, Daddy. I stabbed him with Mom's paring knife!" I blurted out. I started to cry again as the fear and helplessness came rushing back. My parents both sat down on my bed then and listened while I relived the whole story, including the part about Mom's paring knife. Charlie sat up wide-eyed on his own bed and listened as well. I sniffled and cried most of the way through the telling, but even as I went on with my story, I could feel the terrifying events of the evening shifting gradually into a different perspective. I was calming down, and the warm familiarity of my room began to make our wild flight seem like a bad dream. When I finally finished my story, I swiped my nose on my sleeve and asked, "Daddy, will I get in trouble for stabbing Mr. Sherwood? Do you think Chief Galsworthy knows about it?"

My dad put his hand on my head and stroked my hair. "Well, even if the Chief knows, you're not in trouble, Sweetie. The law says that if someone tries to hurt you, you get to fight back. It's called 'self-defense'."

With my dad's reassurance, I felt suddenly, crushingly, exhausted. Charlie had listened raptly to my account, but now he, too, seemed overcome by the evening's events. He slid down beneath his covers and sighed deeply.

Mom kissed us both and said, "I'm going to drive out to the hospital to see if I can do anything for Robert's mom. Daddy will be right here if you need him. We'll leave the hall light on, and the entryway light, too, so if you want us for anything in the night, just come down and...oh, I know, I'll bring you the sick bell."

The sick bell was an old cowbell that we got to keep by our bedside when we were sick. We rang it when we needed help or when we wanted something. I knew Mom was concerned that we might wake up and be too frightened to go downstairs to get help. I knew, too, that having the cowbell within reach in the night would be almost as comforting as having Mom or Dad sleeping right in our room

Our parents got up and, after a few final pats and tucks, left our little bedroom to go downstairs. At the door, Daddy turned back and said, "I'll be right downstairs in the living room. G'nite, kids. Love you." He turned out the light.

On ordinary nights, Charlie and I talked for a while before falling asleep, but that night's conversation was pretty short. After the light had been off for about a minute, Charlie's worried little voice quavered softly, "What will happen to Robert, Lizzie?"

"I don't know." Pause. "I guess his mom will take care of him."

"But you have to have money."

"I know."

We fell asleep.

CHAPTER TWENTY-EIGHT

We woke up to a Sunday morning. Church bells were ringing through the air from the five churches within earshot of Cayuga Street. I could always pick out the Westminster chimes of my own church, and for a moment or two, I lay relaxed and sleepy, lulled by the particular peace of a summer Sunday. Then the memory of the previous evening poured over me, and I sat up, my heart pounding. For a minute or two I just froze there, confused and badly frightened. Looking around a little frantically, my eyes came to rest on my sleeping brother. I focused on his small, familiar form, and gradually began to calm down. I looked around at the little sailboats on the blue wallpaper, the toy boxes, the bookcases, the clutter on the floor...everything was in its rightful place. We were safe in our own room, after all, and somewhere in the house were our parents, forming their constant barrier between us and all bad things. After a few more minutes, the quiet, sunlit surroundings began to eclipse the unnatural events of that other day, that other place.

And then my mother appeared in the bedroom doorway. She came in, sat down on the side of my bed, and put her hand on my blanket-covered knee. "Hi, Sweetie. How are you doin' today?"

"Okay, I guess. Is...have you seen Robert?"

Mom didn't answer right away. She stared out the window. I knew she was searching for the right words to explain this new and troubling reality. "Well, Honey, Robert is...first of all, Robert's mom is home from the hospital. She'll be fine. Well, I mean, her head...injury...is okay. Grace is staying over there to help out. Robert's dad, when he fell down in the water, he hit his head on a rock. So he...well, it knocked him out. So he couldn't...he didn't...get up, and his face was in the water."

"Mom, I know he drowned," I said. "But what will happen to Robert?" Then I was seized with a sudden, frightening possibility. "He won't move away, will he?" The thought of daily life without Robert's companionship struck me as so unbearable that it became, for the moment, my first concern. Robert was my soul mate, the mirror in which I recognized myself.

When my mother saw the dismay in my face, I think she saw Robert as well, and tears sprang to her eyes. She put her arms around me. Charlie, wakened by our voices, crawled sleepily from his own bed and climbed into the midst of our hug. The three of us held each other and cried silently for a few minutes.

After a bit, Mom sat back, sniffed one big sniff, and drew in a big breath. "Okay. Now we need to think about Robert and his mom. Even though you kids know that Robert's dad wasn't always very nice, and even though he did a really bad thing last night, he was still Robert's dad. And he was Inez's husband. When bad things happen, people need their friends. And they didn't have very many friends."

"But they have our family, Mom. And Grace, and the other neighbors. And doesn't Robert have a grandma and grandpa?"

"I think Paul's parent are not...in the picture, but Inez's parents and her sister live in Colorado. They didn't visit very often, because they didn't...I guess they didn't get along very well with Paul. But now...."

Mom was lost in thought a moment. Then she gave herself a brisk little pat on the knee, stood up, and said, "Let's go down and have some breakfast. Then you can help me fix some chicken salad for Robert and his mom. I think the Presbyterian Church can survive without us for one Sunday."

Our family spent that morning hovering near one another, reassuring ourselves that we were all still there, still okay, still together. After breakfast Mom started to assemble the things she'd need to make chicken salad. When she opened the silverware drawer, she reached in and rifled around and then stopped suddenly, pulling her hand back. It struck me at the same moment that the paring knife, of course, was missing. Mom glanced in my direction to see if I'd noticed her reaction. Seeing that I was aware of it, she gave me a quick hug and said, "Don't worry, Honey. We can use the steak knives."

That little incident reminded us all, though, that the paring knife was somewhere out there on the path to the lake. And my suspenders had to be somewhere close by. After my mom had set the chicken on to boil, my dad said matter-of-factly, "Well, Mom, I think I'll just go out and retrieve that knife and Lizzie's suspenders." I knew this was an open invitation...I could go with him or stay home, whichever I felt I needed to do.

He paused a moment, rumpled my hair, and went out the door. At first I felt relief that he'd gone without me, but as I stood there, it occurred to me that I would inevitably want to go down that sidewalk to the lake again, and it might be better to do it now, in broad daylight, with my dad along.

On an impulse I ran out the door, calling, "Wait, Daddy. I wanna go with you."

"Are you sure? You don't have to, you know."

"I know. I think I know where to look, though."

"Okay. C'mon then, Punkin." My father's voice was easy and light, but he reached down and took my hand, and I let him hang on to it.

When we reached the spot where I thought our scuffle with Mr. Sherwood had taken place, I said, "I think he caught up to us about here, Daddy. Robert fell down by that curb." We looked around on the sidewalk and in the grass.

Almost immediately, my dad bent down and picked something up and turned it over in his hand. Then he leaned down again and made a swiping motion in the grass. He'd found the knife. I didn't realize until later that he'd wiped the blade clean in the grass.

"Well, here's Mom's paring knife," he said, showing it to me. It looked perfectly ordinary in his hand. It seemed impossible that it was the same knife I'd stuck into Mr. Sherwood's leg such a short time ago.

My father was watching me to see how I'd react to the knife, but, for me, it had turned back into Mom's familiar paring knife, the same one that peeled apples and sliced celery and turned the eyes out of potatoes. I guess Dad could see I was doing all right, because he said, "Well, shall we track down those suspenders?"

We looked around the area between the sidewalk and the street, and after only a minute or so, my dad said, "Here we go." He picked up my suspenders and wound them around his hand. Shaking his head he said, "I bet old Hopalong Cassidy would be surprised to hear what these suspenders have been up to."

"Yeah, I guess so." I managed a shaky grin.

187

"Well, we've got the knife and the suspenders. Did you lose anything else, Lizzie?"

I looked around in the grass. There, a few inches from the base of a big maple tree, lay a small rectangle of chamois cloth, still taped together with adhesive tape. I picked it up, feeling sheepish and uncomfortable. "This was the sheath. I guess the knife flew out of it."

My dad reached out his hand. "Can I see it?"

I handed it over. He turned it over a few times in his hand. "Nice job, Lizzie. Very...creative." He paused. "I guess you really wanted that knife, didn't you." It was a statement, not a question.

"Well, I don't want it anymore!" As I said this, I was surprised to realize it was true.

Dad laughed and said, "Your mama will be glad to hear that!" He put the sheath in his pocket. He looked off toward the lake, and he looked thoughtfully at me. "How about we walk down to the lake. I think it's time somebody else got a look at this cave of yours, don't you?"

My father and I continued on down the sidewalk, retracing the path Robert and I had taken the night before. Of course, it wasn't the same journey at all, transformed as it was by the effects of daylight, the comforting presence of my father, and the absence of fear. I'm baffled, now, by the ease with which I had distanced myself from the events of the previous evening, even from the fact of Mr. Sherwood's drowning. It is the gift of children to live in the present, I suppose. I was eight years old, and I'd never really known anyone who had died. I wasn't thinking about the way my friend Robert's life would be forever altered. Walking along in the sunshine with my father, I really felt quite nearly happy.

When we reached the steps leading down to the dock, though, I did feel the shadow of the previous night brush over me. I looked down at the water lapping lazily across the sand. I could see how shallow it was. I could see the rocks that scattered the shoreline and protruded, moss-covered and slippery, out of the water near the shore. I was trying to picture Robert's dad lying there, face down and still.

"Does it hurt to drown, Daddy?" I blurted.

My father looked startled, then sad. He put his arm around my shoulders. "Well, Honey, Mr. Galsworthy thinks that Mr. Sherwood tripped and fell in the water and hit his head real hard on a rock. He had a pretty bad cut by his forehead. That probably knocked him out, at least. That's why he didn't get up. He probably never felt anything, really."

"Daddy?"

"Hmmm?"

I was afraid to ask, but I needed to know. "Do you think he could have tripped because he had a knife cut on his leg?"

I could tell that my dad considered this a serious question—an important question. He turned to face me and leaned down and put his hands on my shoulders. "No, Honey. He fell because he was drunk and it was dark and there were slippery rocks in the water. I'm sure when you stuck him, he felt it for a minute, and that gave you and Robert time to get away. That was a good thing. A very good thing. But there's one advantage to being drunk like Paul Sherwood, and that is you don't feel pain so much. So that little knife stick you gave him wasn't bothering him at all by the time he got as far as the lake."

I was satisfied with that. I let go of my small edge of guilt. Daddy and I went down the steps, and I showed him our cave. He bent forward and glanced into the small, clay-lined cubbyhole. Then he turned and looked down at the shore, measuring the distance from one to the other. After a minute he straightened and said, "Yup, that's one very special cave. And I won't tell anyone else where it is, Lizzie."

"That's okay, Daddy. I don't think we'll want to play in it anymore. Not for a long time, anyway."

My dad held out his hand to me. "Shall we go home now?"

CHAPTER TWENTY-NINE

We walked back together, my father holding my hand. When we reached our driveway, we found the police chief's car parked behind our station wagon. Chief Galsworthy and my mother must have been on the lookout for us, because they came out on the back porch to meet us. The chief was wearing ordinary clothes instead of his uniform, I suppose because it was a Sunday, but he looked a lot less like a policeman and quite a bit less important. He seemed a little uncomfortable standing there on our porch, and his discomfort made me feel oddly embarrassed and a bit nervous. I knew he was going to have to ask me some questions, and I worried whether I would know the answers. After an awkward little pause, my dad said, "Let's go in and have some lemonade, John." He didn't let go of my hand, not even when we sat down at the kitchen table. Mom bustled around, getting out glasses and ice cubes and lemonade. Chief Galsworthy took a long drink and then put his glass down on the table. For a minute, he stared down at the glass, turning it around between his hands. I watched his glass, too, noticing that even though the glass was turning, the ice cubes weren't, and I wondered why.

Mr. Galsworthy took another drink, set the glass back down, and said solemnly, "Lizzie, I guess you know about Robert's dad."

"Yes, sir," I responded. I rarely used the word "sir," so I must have felt the gravity of the interview.

"Well, we know it was an accident. We know it wasn't anybody's fault." Pause. "Well, actually, it was probably his own fault. Anyway, I have to write a report about it, so I just have to make sure I know exactly what happened, you know, so I can get it right in my report."

I felt a little chill of concern. My dad had assured me I couldn't get in trouble over stabbing Mr. Sherwood, but maybe Dad didn't know. Maybe he had just been trying to make me feel better. A kid named Martin Flinders had once brought a sharp knife to school, and the principal had called the police to come and take it away and give Martin a good talking-to, and that had been for just *having* a knife. I glanced over at Dad. He seemed businesslike and calm. He gave my hand a squeeze.

Mr. Galsworthy continued, "Your mom showed me that little window in your attic that looks down into Robert's kitchen, so I know how you saw Mr. Sherwood going after

Inez…going after Mrs. Sherwood, and then after Robert. So, do you remember what happened next?"

"Well, I ran down the stairs…," I started out nervously, but the Chief just nodded quietly, looking interested, and my insides settled down. I repeated the story, then, while my family heard it all for the second time, and Mr. Galsworthy kept nodding and uttering an occasional "umhum" and jotting down a few notes in his little spiral notebook. When I got to the part about sticking Mr. Sherwood in the leg, my dad interrupted, "Oh, here's the knife, John. We found it this morning in the grass by the sidewalk. And…here are Lizzie's suspenders. They were there, too." Dad got up to gather the knife and my suspenders from the counter where he'd laid them.

Silently, Mr. Galsworthy turned the knife over in his hand, and then he gave my suspenders a poke with his finger. He looked at me curiously. I suppose he could tell I was a little uneasy, because he said, "Now, Lizzie, you're not in any trouble here. Do you understand that? In fact, you were very brave. Nobody is blaming you for anything that happened. Do you believe me?"

"Yeah, I guess so. I mean, yes, sir."

"But the thing is, I'm just a little confused about…what I don't quite get…I know you had this paring knife hooked up somehow? Could you show me? I don't have to put this in my report. I'm just getting things clear in my own head."

Embarrassed, I picked up my suspenders and showed him how I'd wrapped them around my leg. I was wearing shorts that morning, and I was acutely aware of how the suspenders looked, now that they weren't covered by my pant leg. "I had long pants on yesterday," I mumbled, looking down at my leg.

The Chief wasn't laughing at me, though. In fact, he seemed pretty fascinated by the whole little spectacle playing out before him. Reassured, I went on, "And then I had the knife in this sheath I made out of chamois, and I had it all strapped in like this...." I showed him how I had tucked the knife down inside the snug web of suspender straps. My dad pulled the sheath from his pocket and offered it to the Chief, who examined it with interest.

Looking from the sheath to the suspenders wrapped around my leg, the chief shook his head and said, "Hmmm, pretty ingenious, Miss Elizabeth." He stood up and put his hands on his hips, a gesture which was considerably less impressive when he was wearing street clothes than when his hips were encased in his thick leather uniform belt with the revolver slung on one side. "I don't know that I believe in miracles, but I know a piece of real good luck when I see it."

Something was still itching away at the back of my mind. "Mr. Galsworthy, my dad says that if somebody's trying to hurt you, it's okay to stick them with your knife if you have to. Like if there's no other choice?"

The chief rocked back and forth on his heels while he thought about this. I don't think he was used to dealing with eight-year-olds in his line of work, and he seemed anxious to handle things correctly. "'Well, yes," he finally said. "If you're really in trouble. Of course, it's best if you can manage to stay out of trouble in the first place. But I'd say that, considering the situation that you and Robert were in, you did exactly what you needed to do. I guess some people might even think you're a little bit of a hero."

I felt my face turning hot. I didn't feel like a hero, and I was guilt-ridden over anyone else even entertaining the idea. Heroes, in my estimation, didn't run away in terror, they didn't cower in caves, and they certainly didn't wet their pants. I hoped with all my heart that the Chief didn't know about that last thing.

I stared uncomfortably at the floor. Mr. Galsworthy put his big hand on my head and said kindly, "Don't worry, Lizzie. You did a fine job helping me figure out what happened. Now I won't have to bother your friend Robert with a bunch of questions. That'd be the last thing he needs right now."

The Chief shook my dad's hand and nodded in my mom's direction. "Well, thanks, folks. I won't need much more here. Probably stop by in a few days with a written statement. Take care of this little cowgirl here." He smiled a tired smile and went out the screen door, no doubt dreading his next stop across the back yard.

CHAPTER THIRTY

After he left, Mom stood for a minute looking blankly after him. Then she kind of came to and went back to the stove where the chicken was simmering. She picked out a little bit of chicken with a fork, blew on it gently, and tasted it. Turning off the burner, she said, "Lizzie, when we get this chicken salad put together, I'm going to take it next door so they can have it for lunch if they want to. You don't have to go with me unless you want to. Robert and Inez are going to be very sad and tired, but people show sadness in all kinds of ways. They might be crying, but they might not be. Robert might want to be in his room alone, or he might want a friend to talk to. But, however they want to be, it's fine, okay? So...do you think you'd like to go with me, Honey?" My mother was being careful not to put pressure on me. She fussed with the chicken salad, adding pickles and eggs and grapes and mayonnaise and other things while she talked.

The truth was, I didn't really want to go, but I felt guilty for my reluctance. And I was a little curious, too. The whole situation over at Robert's house seemed weird and intensely uncomfortable. Then it occurred to me that Robert, my best friend Robert, had no choice about being there.

"Well, I guess I'll go. But what do I say? How do I act?"

Mom could tell I was asking for specific directions, not empty reassurance. "I tell you what, Lizzie. Why don't you just stay right by me until we kind of see how things are going. There will probably be some other people there, too. People usually gather around to help at times like this. You won't have to say a thing unless you want to."

That reassured me, and I stood up to go with Mom. She gave the chicken salad a last stir and covered it with a little elasticized bowl cover. I held the screen for her, and we crossed the yard together. I climbed the porch steps and knocked self-consciously on the Sherwoods' kitchen door. In a moment, Grace appeared and opened it.

"Oh, Lizzie. Hi, Marian. Oh, how nice. That looks wonderful. It's your special recipe with the grapes, isn't it, Marian. Let's put it right here on the counter. You know what, Lizzie? I'm going to get Robert. He's just sitting in the living room talking to Mrs. Krebb, but I think Mrs. Krebb is doing all the talking. His mom is upstairs having a little rest. I think Robert would rather be out on the porch with you."

It was confusing to me, seeing Grace act like everything was under control. I almost wanted to shout, "His father is dead!" At the same time, it was a relief to feel that grown-ups were still calmly functioning, still suggesting what I should do. I watched with some fascination as Grace and two or three other women quietly moved about the kitchen, competently fixing food, writing down telephone messages, finding utensils in drawers they'd never opened before, and cleaning up after themselves. I wondered how they knew what they were supposed to do. I'd never really studied my mother in a situation like this, either, but now I saw how seamlessly she moved into the little network of efficient helpfulness. It was oddly comforting, and I felt proud of her.

Grace came back into the kitchen, followed by a wan and solemn Robert. Promising a treat for us, she steered Robert and me out to the back steps. Darting momentarily back into the kitchen, she reappeared carrying a plate of cookies and two bottles of orange pop. "Here you go, kids. I doubt anyone will bother you out here on the back porch. People are coming up the front steps, you know. If anyone stops by, just send them on up into the kitchen. Robert, we'll have some lunch in an hour or so. Lizzie's mom brought chicken salad."

And with that, Grace disappeared back into the kitchen. Robert and I sat there without speaking, both of us feeling awkward and embarrassed. We listened to the soft, almost cheerful cadence of the women's voices drifting out from the kitchen. I felt our silence extending uncomfortably, so I shoved the cookie plate closer to Robert and said, "You want one? They look like the kind Mrs. Krebb makes. They've got chocolate chips and walnuts."

"Sure," Robert answered quietly. He took a cookie and bit into it, chewed thoughtfully and said, "I guess you know about my dad and ...everything."

"Yeah," I answered. Knowing I should add something, I said, "I'm real sorry, Robert."

"Yeah," he said, looking down at the steps. We both munched on our cookies for a minute or so, avoiding each other's eyes. Then Robert spoke up. "My dad's old job place called. They said they were gonna pretend my dad wasn't...that he still worked there, so my mom will get some money from his company."

I had no idea what Robert was talking about, but I knew money was important, so I nodded and said, "Yeah. I guess that's good, huh? That'll help and everything?"

"I guess so. My mom cried on the phone when they called."

I glanced sideways at Robert. He was crying now, too...not sobbing, but just sitting there, motionless, while tears rolled silently down his cheeks and dropped unnoticed into his lap. He had stopped chewing. He held the rest of his cookie in his hand, resting it on one knee, but he had forgotten it. He stared at his feet, seeing nothing.

Then I realized with some amazement that I was crying too. It was probably the first time in my life that I had cried tears of empathy. I looked at my friend sitting there, fragile and crumpled with the weight of his grief, and I forgot my discomfort and embarrassment. I slid over next to him and put my arm around his shoulders. He sat motionless for a moment, and then he let his head tip slowly down against my neck. His hair was warm from the sun. We sat there for a long time, soothed by the summer sunlight and the reassuring drone of conversation wafting over us from the kitchen. Eventually Robert's tears slowed, and then stopped. The scents of honeysuckle and cut grass curled around us, and high in the belfry of the Presbyterian Church, the Westminster chimes sounded the hour.

EPILOGUE

After the accidental drowning of Mr. Sherwood, Robert and his mother were adopted by the neighborhood and by the wider community in a way that they never had been when Mr. Sherwood was alive. I could never decide if it was because they felt guilty, or if Mr. Sherwood's death eliminated the whole question of abuse from people's social equations. Folks might not quite know where to place a woman who got knocked around by her husband, but they knew exactly where to place a tragic widow and her small child. Neighbors began dropping by with sweet corn and strawberries and brownies. My aunts dropped off boys' clothes that my older boy cousins had outgrown. My dad and Mr. Hibbs and his two teenage sons helped out with yard care and house repairs.

As Dad had once suggested, Mom invited Robert's mother to join her women's club. And as Mom had predicted, Mrs. Sherwood declined, but said she appreciated being asked.

In the fall of that year, Mrs. Sherwood found a job as the receptionist at the new three-doctor clinic on the west side of town. (She took a taxi for three weeks, until my mom finally convinced her that she could learn to drive their car. Mom was a good teacher, but she said she was relieved when Mrs. Sherwood passed her driving test on the first try.) Robert just stayed at our house when we weren't in school, which wasn't that much of a change from before. Grace stepped in as babysitter whenever she got the chance.

At the clinic, Mrs. Sherwood ran the front desk efficiently and cheerfully, and when Barbara Cortland, the office manager, retired to spend more time with her teenage kids (who were running wild, according to the neighborhood gossip), Mrs. Sherwood stepped up to that position. I think she really liked working. She met lots of people, and she kept busy, and the doctors told her frequently that the office had never run so smoothly. When she got her promotion, she invited my mother and me over for coffee and lemonade. It was the first time she'd ever invited my mom into their house on a weekend.

As for Robert, he was quiet and sad through July and August, but as summer faded and cooled into fall, and fall into winter, his grief gradually transformed into a reflective calm. His mother's newfound contentment settled down over Robert like a comforting blanket. He and I spent a lot of time together after school and on Saturdays, but for a long time, we left our games of fantasy and imagination behind. We read comics and played Parcheesi and roamed the neighborhood, but we never pretended to be anyone other than who we were.

And then one sunny Saturday afternoon in mid-December, Robert and I were sitting on my living room floor looking at the toy section of the Sears and Roebuck catalog when my mother came in and said, "Lizzie, why don't you and Robert go up in the attic and dig out the Christmas tree decorations and bring them down. We're getting our tree later if Dad has time."

Robert and I looked at each other. We hadn't played in the attic since my birthday. An overwhelming flood of memories, good and bad, washed over me. I could see in Robert's face the same conflicting emotions. But we were, in the end, still children, and the lure of our attic Neverland was still sweet and powerful. We got up from the floor and linked our hands together and headed for the stairs. We climbed slowly and deliberately, realizing that this was a pilgrimage. When we reached the little window of colored glass, I looked out, but saw only a snowy lawn and a lighted window across the way.

At the top of the stairs we stopped and looked across the long silent space of the attic. The dim, hazy light from the window outlined the maze of boxes and trunks and old furniture. I'd forgotten how the winter attic smelled...woody and dry and dusty. It wasn't especially cold, as the day had been unusually warm and bright. The boxes and boards that comprised our pirate ship and the rest of Neverland stood untouched in the center of the attic. They just looked like boxes and boards. Robert and I stood looking at the scene for a minute or so. Finally, uneasy in our quiet contemplation, I said, "It's not the same, is it?"

Robert shook his head. "No, it's not the same."

We looked a minute longer. Then, with a sigh, I said, "Well, let's go find the end of the lights and look for the decorations." We circled around the refrigerator crate and the board we'd used as a plank and the rest of the boxes that had made up our magic kingdom. We stepped over the lagoon and went past the Indian tepee. I followed the string of Christmas lights over to the far wall where we'd plugged them in. Reaching down for the end of the string, I heard Robert say, "Hang on a second, Lizzie." He paused. "Just plug them in once."

"Okay," I shrugged, and wiggled the plug into the outlet.

I stood and glanced over at my friend. A little half-smile was playing about his lips. His eyes shone with the reflection of dozens of lights. "Look at it now, Lizzie," he said softly.

I turned and looked back at our ship. I don't know why the lights made such a difference. Maybe Robert and I just needed to be drawn back to a place we wanted to be...a place we had been missing. Anyway, the glow from the Christmas bulbs cast itself over the pirate ship, outlining it, defining it, changing it from a dark and colorless collection of crates and boxes into a softly gleaming fantasy. The pole became a mast again, the big crate turned into a ship's hull. The plank called out for daring, last-second rescues. Metallic door pulls and bits of glass and ceramic scattered about the attic sparkled with reflections of red, blue, green, and gold. The lagoon and the tree house and all the rest of Neverland emerged from the shadowy corners. Dust motes twinkled like stars.

I looked back at Robert. We smiled at each other. Robert spoke, ever so quietly, "I get to be Peter Pan!"

CPSIA information can be obtained at www.ICGtesting.com
Printed in the USA
BVOW01s0909100414

350165BV00001B/248/P